The
Helena
Orbit

Books from Lillicat Publishers

Visions Anthology Series
Visions: Leaving Earth
Visions II: Moons of Saturn
Visions III: Inside the Kuiper Belt
Visions IV: Space Between Stars
Visions V: Milky Way
Visions VI: Galaxies
Visions VII: Universe (2017)

Northern Futures
TreeVolution
The Future Is Short: Science Fiction in a Flash
The Future Is Short, Volume 3: Science Fiction in a Flash

Dance With Me: My Journey Through Cancer
Sunshine & Shadow: Memories from a Long Life

ROGUE STAR PRESS
The Helena Orbit

DAWN LIGHT PRESS
The Night Blooming Jasmine in Your Heart

ALTERNATE UNIVERSE PRESS
Snake in the Grass (2017)

The
Helena
Orbit

James Dunham

Rogue Star Press
USA

"Water Night" by Octavio Paz, translated by Muriel Rukeyser, from *Early Poems 1933-1955*, copyright ©1973 by Octavio Paz and Muriel Rukeyser. Reprinted by permission of New Directions Publishing Corp.

www.lillicatpublishers.com
www.roguestarpress.com

First Print Edition: May 2017

Print ISBN: *978-1-945646-16-4*
EPUB ISBN: *978-1-945646-17-1*
MOBI ISBN: *978-1-945646-18-8*

To my mentors:
Tom, Gary, Catherine, Glen, Lawrence, Mike, and
Wendell

Your help carried me light years

Contents

Acknowledgements

This writing was manifestly a collaborative process, and particular people deserve explicit mention for helping to make this novel what it is.

First I must thank those who read drafts throughout the writing process and gave me useful feedback, including my family and especially my brother John and sisters Catherine and Cynthia, and my father, Stephen: thanks for sharing your reactions and ideas for improvement. Thanks as well to people who generously agreed to read later drafts under deadline, and gave such detailed and insightful responses: Lee Davis, Melissa Goodrich, and Kenny Lakes, you're the best.

Energetic thanks to Norman Hill for acting as my detector of egregious scientific implausibility and helping me to steer my fictional machinations in at least the general direction of the believable—Norman, your enthusiasm, generosity of time, and breadth of useful knowledge are vastly appreciated.

Thank you as well to Carrol Fix at Lillicat Publishers for seeing so much value in my work, editing it thoughtfully, and taking a chance on a first novel by an unknown author.

To my friends in the writing vocation who have encouraged me over the years, thank you. I couldn't have written this novel without having spent significant time with my fellow fiction MFA-ers Amy Denham, Amy Mckenzie, Misha Rai, and Eric Schlich—thank you all for challenging me. To my fellow graduates of the SU Writers Institute, especially Elizabeth Deanna Morris Lakes, thank you—simply engaging in a discussion about writing or offering a positive word here and there has made all the difference.

Thank you beyond words to the teachers to whom this book is dedicated—I owe you all more than I can say.

The resolution of the novel owes a great deal to the music of Eric Whitacre and the poetry of Octavio Paz, without whose beautiful works I wouldn't have been able to write the penultimate chapter. Thank you to Elisabeth Daumer and William Rukeyser for your assistance, and to New Directions Publishing for granting reprint permission. I hope a choir still performs "Water Night" half a millennium from now, on this planet or some other.

And to Kristin, my friendlier and more compassionate half, an infinity of gratitude. Infinity squared.

One

In my dreams I feel her turn.

The *Euclid*, our home, our colony. The closest we've had to a planet until today.

Someone at the great ship's helm makes a course correction, and the nanograv flooring and walls should render the inertia negligible, but halfway awake, I dream that my legs become too heavy to lift, and I look up to see the dream stars above me change direction, the dark horizon tilt to one side, my body slipping into freefall. I wake and keep still, so motionless I can't be sure I'm not still dreaming: the speed and spin of space surge through my arms and legs, and I am an asteroid, rotating on multiple axes at once, hurtling through the open black. A thruster fires on the bow of the ship, and it angles, perfects its trajectory toward the destination of our mobile colony's five-hundred-year journey.

While I lie here in bed half-dreaming, much of the ship's population already stands at the windows or sits in the domes, watching our strange new home grow larger: the planet 51 Pegasi h. Helena. A crescent of maroon and gray hung slim on the starfield. These last two school years, I've stopped at windows and swelled a little inside to see the planet grow larger every day. Today it will stretch to fill our windows from top to bottom. Today, after cruising through the emptiest space for five centuries, only the last eighteen years of which I've lived to see, today we enter orbit.

The course correction ends. The silence and blank, default-gray walls of my empty room fail to put me back to sleep. I give up trying. I step off my bed to the floor, and use the keypad on the side of the polymer mattress to deflate it into a dense all-purpose marble which I adhere to the waistband of my pajama shorts.

I don't feel like deciding what dress to wear to the Orbit Day ceremony yet, but I do want to see where we are, not just feel it in some buried motion sensitivity I don't seem to have when I'm awake. So I take the marble that was my bed and inflate it into a sphere large enough to stand inside. I enter it with a hatch, and once through, with the door closed behind me and the only light coming from a square grid of dots on the floor, I touch a few keys on my waistband. The sphere connects to the ship's wi-fi, and the inside surface of the sphere displays visual readout in every direction. I see into space as if I am the *Euclid* herself, one of my favorite ways to remind myself what my home is and what lies beyond it. Above me, stars. Below me, stars.

I turn around and gasp. My knees give way and drop me to the floor.

51 Pegasi h floats even larger than I expected, taller than I am, so tall and wide I can see her archipelagos without a telescope. We've passed other planets in this system in the past two years, but none so close as this, the one we hope to someday call home. Here she is.

Helena.

We are close enough now to see mountain ranges on her brown and purple continents, layers of cloud above her pale seas. Nearly close enough to see the life we know exists here. Shallow vegetation, but no animals yet seen, at least on land. That may soon change.

Here on my knees, while I wait, she grows larger right in front of me, her horizons visibly expanding in only seconds. Waxing from a crescent into a half-circle as we approach her sunside, lit by her ancient star, a sun small and white like Sol but millions of years more mature.

I can't stay here any longer. I open the sphere, and it shrinks back down to a marble. I touch my waistband and key in a change of clothes, stand up, and let my pajamas change into an Earth dress, a skinsuit underneath to scrub the night's sweat off me while I brush my hair. I keep waiting for someone to develop an automatic comb so that I don't have to spend so much time on my appearance, but such a project isn't too high on any of the engineers' priority lists.

I'm sure my parents have already left for the nearest dome, but my grandparents and great-grandmother may still be sleeping. It's two hours before my alarm, three before we're scheduled to enter orbit.

I'm hungry, but the farms and cafeterias are closed for the day, so I order a nutrition bar from the recombined-matter dispenser in the wall. While I eat, I set the marble on its full-length mirror setting and look myself over. My hair, black and tangled, needs more brushing. The skinsuit is fading, almost finished cleaning, and my dress looks appropriately festive and colorful, a welcome change from my labwear. I do a little hop when I remember I get to wear cute shoes today, and I get my shoe-marble and its keypad from a drawer in the wall. I flip up the keypad's mini screen and scroll through the various pairs I've programmed into it until I find one that matches my dress: equally as colorful, even on the ergonomic treads, with a completely useless little bow on top of the toe. I love it.

My friends tease me sometimes about my excitement over looking pretty on special occasions, and I blame it on my unusually traditional mother, who believes that one's looks say a lot about a person. She can spend in excess of an hour trying on various combinations of clothes, shoes, and even jewelry to wear for a big event. She has three full marbles for clothes alone, not counting shoes, which I admit is pretty extreme. Friends ask her if she feels insecure, to fixate on appearance so much, but she tells them appearance is a lost art, and she walks the corridors of the ship with an air of complete confidence. When she wears her work face, I keep my distance.

Happy with how I look now, I step through the automatic doors of my family's home and into the corridor. The ceilings are still dark, the corridor lit dimly by lights at the bottoms of the walls, the simulated dawn still hours away. All the ship's architecture echoes Earth, a planet I've seen only in virtual reality, read about in history class, watched in old obsolete-format video. A mere memory. The scents and textures in the simulation are conjecture, based on chemical records and artifacts. The ceilings of our hallways mimic the blue of Earth's sky, our light levels imitate its daily rotation and sun, and the standard gravity setting is one G: Earth. Yet to me it's nothing but the point of human origin. It doesn't hold the nostalgia it does for my grandparents, who themselves knew it no better than I do.

The halls loom, quiet, but when a neighbor from down the corridor, a woman my parents' age, sees me, she rushes over and kisses my cheek.

"Happy Orbit Day, Edwyn," she whispers. "I love your dress. See you at the dome." She hurries down the corridor, and I smile as I watch her go. A few people I don't know pass me going the other direction, and we nod and smile at each other, the excitement hard to contain. Most of my school friends have been awake all night, excited about the day off from classes and the chance to sit back and really see our destination for the first time. They've been looking through the public telescopes and magnified video feeds since yesterday evening, competing to be the first to discover whatever there may be to discover. I stayed up with them until around midnight, but needed to get a least a couple hours' rest before the celebration.

Around the bend the maglev station sits empty. Usually people crowd together waiting for the pods to emerge from the tunnels and take them where they need to go. Today, everyone is already there. A vacant one-person pod waits on the track, and I step into it, sit down, and tell it my destination: the nearest dome, where I expect my family to be. I've forgotten how easy it is, this early in the morning when the pod's lights are low, to see the dim red-lit panels that line the inside of the tunnels, long dark tubes that connect the different areas of the *Euclid* like veins carrying humors to all her corners.

The tunnel walls whisper by until the pod stops at a station and I get out. Voices from the corridor fill the room, and outside a line of people waits to enter the dome. Everyone wears formal clothing, some of them in nice Earth dresses and many in Earth suits, others in clothing of their own design, many-colored, many-paneled, many-layered, nongendered.

A young man I don't know, in line next to me, shakes my hand. "Happy Orbit Day."

I return the greeting. From his face and skin I notice his genes look similar to mine, largely Hispanic. I say, "I'm Edwyn, from the Lower Bow quad."

He nods. "Rio, Lower Stern."

Without his insignia to go by, I'm not sure how old he is. I ask, "Still in Path School?"

"Actually I'm finishing first year of apprenticeship."

"Congrats. I'm graduating Path next week. Any advice?"

"It's a lot more intense than Path."

"That's what everyone says."

"But it's exciting, too. What's your field?"

I feel a twinge of embarrassment. "I'm waiting for the expo. My parents are hoping I'll go for bioengineering." I don't mention that I am already beyond tired of bioengineering, and, like most of my generation, would much rather study the life on Helena. "What's yours?"

"Geology. But every field is going to get exciting after today. I do have one piece of advice: choose a mentor who gets you excited about your research. If you have that, the field doesn't matter, as long as you can learn to be good at it."

This advice runs contrary to what most others have told me, which is that I should choose the field I'm most skilled in. Rio's way of looking at it makes sense, though. Path School is supposed to prepare us for all of the major fields, so in theory, I could become skilled at whatever I choose as long as I stick with it.

We reach the door to the dome. "Thank you," I say. "Nice to meet you."

"Happy Orbit Day," he says again. We go our separate ways, and the further I get into the dome, following the walkway around the hundreds of rows of seating, the more everything falls to a hush. Everyone sits, reverent and transfixed by the planet above them, the dome so clear it is as if they are sitting outside on the hull of the ship, the seats tilted back for comfortable stargazing.

My family and I agreed on where to sit ahead of time, so I find the row. There they wait, my parents and their parents, my maternal uncle and paternal aunt, their spouses, my cousins, and my maternal great-grandmother, our oldest relative. We are a rare sight, many parents these days registering either in groups or as individuals, a lineage of only two-parent pairs for four generations having become uncommon. Overly traditional.

My parents have saved a seat for me next to them. I greet each relative, Happy Orbit Days all around, as I slip by toward my parents, who sit holding hands and staring up at the sky. They turn and smile and stand, each hugging me in turn as if they hadn't just seen me last night. My mother looks at my dress, and a fleeting, fascinated look tells me she has an idea of a way to improve my outfit, but she doesn't mention it, tells me only that I look wonderful. She is wearing a dress she designed especially for today, a royal purple evening gown with matching shoes and earrings, her hair gathered and styled in the back in a complex arrangement of braids that must have taken forever. I tell her she looks good, too. She and my father can't help hugging me again before we sit down.

I watch the planet with them. It is so much larger, even, than when I saw it only a short while ago, ever finer details of its continents visible. It stretches across nearly the entire dome. We have hours, still, until the ceremony, and we sit here content to simply revel in the sight. There has never been a moment like this in our history, and this moment especially has been dreamed of and longed for and imagined by so many generations.

No one who set foot on Earth lived on our *Euclid* more recently than four hundred and fifty years ago, and their great-grandchildren have long since turned to dust after bearing great-grandchildren of their own, who are still ancestors of those who fill the ship's rooms today. My great-grandmother, two seats over from me, was born only a short hundred years ago. To her, Helena was until these past two years as much a fable as Earth. She expected to see the fifty-year deceleration begin, but not to see orbit. Given a choice between her species' birthplace so many generations behind her and a planet she might die before reaching, it's no wonder she longed for where our colony came from rather than where we were going.

Even some of us born in the last twenty years wondered if we would see this day. Five hundred years of carefully selected breeding to maintain a diverse gene pool hadn't stopped strange mutations, new sex chromosomes, or new diseases from emerging. Many of the ship's people possess an inert sex chromosome called the "human Z chromosome," whose emergence halfway through the voyage further complicated the colony's ideas of gender. My friend Haruko, also the most famous musician aboard, lives under constant observation to make sure a sudden and anomalous skin condition doesn't kill her.

In a short while, Haruko, the youngest person to hold the title of Artist Laureate of the *Euclid*, will rise from her seat in the orchestra dome and conduct her latest formal composition. Her skin is fragile enough from the condition that this level of activity may injure her, and she will be connected to several medical support systems to make sure the skin on her arms or neck and shoulders does not split open while she conducts.

She will not care. This is what she lives for. This is what we all live for, what we have all been living to see.

#

The ceremony begins with an announcement over the intercom: "Attention citizens. This is Adjo Themba, Captain of *Euclid* Operations Crew speaking. In approximately twenty-five minutes, our colony vessel is scheduled to enter orbit above the planet you see before you, 51 Pegasi h, or, affectionately, Helena. In commemoration of these last moments in our long, long journey, I am proud to introduce Haruko Kanno, our colony's Artist Laureate. Today she is going to conduct for you the *Euclid* Symphony Orchestra as they perform her composition 'Symphony in E minor,' composed over the past two years especially for this occasion.

"Liner notes are available on the network for any who wish to read along, but it is the composer's intent that the piece be heard while reflecting on where we have come from, where we have been along the way, and where we are going. That, she says, will be more than enough explanation. The start of the performance has been timed so that the composition's final movement will reach its apex at the moment we are scheduled to attain stable orbit above the planet, marking the official end of the *Euclid's* five-hundred-year journey from the moon Io to this beautiful planet you see. Please welcome the maestro."

The applause deafens, but out of respect for timing and unquenchable anticipation it quickly dies down. Utter silence falls as the orchestra finishes a final tuning check, that resonant A-pitch unifying the instruments and suggesting the magnitude of the symphony to come. Imagining her in the orchestra dome, I can nearly feel Haruko standing, eyes closed, breathing, and then raising her arms.

The symphony starts with a rolling rumble of timpani and bass drum, like the echo of distant thunder on the far side of an Earth mountain. Having known Haruko all through her composition of the piece, I have it nearly memorized. The drums gradually quiet, symbolizing an end to the turmoil of the late twenty-first century on Earth, as civilization nearly extinguished itself in the pursuit of individual achievement. Out of the echo of the thunder rises a pair of cellos, playing a repeating, major-key up-and-down motif in perfect unison, the pair alone at first, but with other pairs gradually joining: violas, double-basses, violins, until the entire string section bounces with the rhythm, each pair of instruments providing its own subtle harmonic line but fused in time. Even those who don't know Haruko can recognize the reference to the Second Enlightenment, the birth of Earth's collaborative economy that brought it out of the socially stratified, war-torn era of money and competition.

Echoing trumpets and fluttering flutes and piccolos join in, adding a set of high, sailing descants above the dancing strings, humanity's progress accelerating under the new system and breaking technological barriers. French horns and oboes pick up a slower melody in between the strings and high notes, the drums return triumphantly subsumed into the rhythm, and for a moment, the music is overwhelming in its strength and emotion, swelling with the one moment in history when humanity seemed to have found its perfect chord.

Helena has grown so large now that I have to look back and forth to see all of her. The ship begins to turn, and the planet to move ever so slowly downward in our vision. We're maneuvering toward orbit.

The music finishes its first movement with a sweeping, intense minute where the orchestra seems to play five or six compositions at once, tonally blended so as to be easy on the ear. Humanity has spread from Earth to Mars to Ganymede to Callisto, the first colonies, bringing life to dead worlds. Then the music drops back to the original pair of cellos, still energetic but slowing their rhythm, slowing until they draw a final, resolving note.

After a brief silence, the second movement startles with a painful shriek of those same two cellos in a discordant split-second pair of tones. The drums return, with tubas and double-basses in an ominous, militaristic beat that marches, punctuated by those occasional wailing strings and now frantic and sporadic flutes and trombones, a portrait of what can only be the hellish landscape of Io: volcanoes erupting magma over the surface and plumes high into the ragged atmosphere, a cacophony of geological activity so constant and severe that the surface features of the moon change radically from month to month.

A single, quiet oboe plays a mournful dirge, interrupted rhythmically and tonally by the chaos of the Io instruments, making clear the oboe is humanity circling above Io. The oboe finishes its dirge and begins it over. Here was a stationary research colony, in orbit, always in orbit, never sending anything living or valuable to the surface, trapped in the endless freefall that kept it circling this moon of Jupiter. The dirge repeats again. Only above Io did the colonists live the same day over and over. Aboard other orbital colonies above Venus, Europa, and Titan, the colonists found ways to theorize and make progress toward, if not eventual terraforming, at least eventual insulated surface colonies or eventual discovery of life. Above Io, despite the scientists' hopes, orbit was permanent. There could not ever be a surface colony. There could not ever be life.

A single, beautiful note struck firmly in the middle keys of a piano quiets the oboe. Again, the same note, and now one of the instruments of Io fades out. Every ten or fifteen seconds the note again silences another instrument. The dissonance of Io is too the dissonance of the colonists, and someone is calming them down. The piano note becomes an octave, a chain of octaves, gaining breadth and volume as the other sounds cease. One by one, the colonists are deciding to leave. Not to go back to Earth, but to a world of their own.

The orchestra drops away, leaving the piano solo, and the octaves end. The hands of the pianist begin a flurry of activity, segueing between melodies and motifs in different styles. Together, the colonists are planning, designing, drafting a new way of life. A clarinet joins in as the colonists invite scientists from other colonies to help in their endeavor of building the first truly mobile colony, a colony vessel. A single muted trumpet joins the ensemble, and a plucked bass fills out the sound. They are improvising, innovating, discovering a strange, subtle hope.

And in response to their hope, a second ensemble joins, violas and French horns, restating one of the melodies from the first movement's finale, then morphing into this new, unique tune, supporting it. A third ensemble again echoes the music of the collaborative economy, then adds its flutes and trumpets to the new song. The other colonies are helping to make the *Euclid* a reality. They are testing hypotheses, revising potential systems of operation and governance, contributing components and findings from their own research. Various instruments take turns with improvised solos until the second movement finishes in a grand, majestic, jazzy theme, a composite of pieces from the first and second movements transmuted into a coherent whole and enlivened by the addition of the piano and the improvisational style. The *Euclid* has been completed.

The third and final movement subdues the piano, patiently, playing a more emotional, introspective version of the melody that now represents the *Euclid* as it launches and leaves behind Earth's solar system and heads for interstellar space. A soulful baritone sax picks up the melody with slight variations while the piano continues on. At the end of a few phrases, a quirky violin further varies on the melody, and when a bassoon adds a fourth layer, the piano drops out. The melody continues, mutating and reforming in the layers of a lengthy counterpoint which gradually jumps through most of the melodic instruments in the orchestra: an instrument for each generation, down through five hundred years.

The planet Helena has fallen so low in our vision that we can see only the top quarter of her sphere, and she has grown so large that looking to either side does not give us the edge of her. Here, as the counterpoint runs out of iterations, the music acknowledges her approach with two instruments not heard before now: a harp and a hammered dulcimer playing a slow, minor-key duet full of mythos and longing and something unknown.

This was the section of the symphony with which Haruko struggled most. How to portray a planet we don't yet know? She studied the telescope images, sat for long hours in the orchestra dome with replicas of ancient staff paper and ink pen in her hand, and stared at the planet, searching for a melody, sleeping in the angled seat until she saw Helena in her dreams. These night visions gave her the melody. She woke barely able to contain herself enough to write it down, and she played it over and over on the piano until her arms could no longer hold up her hands and she was sure she could never forget it.

The performance of the melody covers me with goosebumps, and when a single, lonesome viola adds a descant I begin to tear up. The whole of the string section swells with supporting sustained notes, and echoes of the Io colony oboe, a muted trumpet, and those original two cellos, filled with yearning and hope. They stir me inside until I have to close my eyes and let them flow, because we are the first generation who has not had to live with true doubt.

We have been the first to know, for certain, that we would arrive at our destination, that nothing could still go wrong to prevent us from getting here. There have been a hundred thousand ways and reasons we might have failed, but we who were born in the last twenty years did not have time to believe the odds were against us. Our parents were told, when they were children, that they would see the new world in their lifetime. But they knew that in fifty years, anything could happen. Our grandparents were told that they might just get to see it if they lived long enough, but they knew better than to hold onto such a remote chance. Our great-grandparents were told only that they might be the last in the very long succession of generations who gave everything for a future they would not see.

Only the children, of whom I must admit I am still one, do not see the planet below as a savior, a release, a burden lifted from weary hearts. Only we children can look at the planet and ask, what next? We are the first for whom Helena is not a journey's end as much as a beginning. How different this makes us from our parents, we cannot understand, for we have the future here in front of us, not millions or billions of kilometers away, or even, incomprehensibly, light years.

I cannot imagine what the first generation to set foot on the *Euclid* must have felt. They were leaving hell behind. Was that enough? Did they not need to arrive? Neither can I fully imagine the tenacity of the intermediate generations, who lived to see neither origin nor destination.

I can only listen while those original two cellos draw out one final, almost endlessly held note, and go quiet. I can only look up and see the multitude of people now weeping around me as the captain announces that we have entered stable orbit. I can only look at my great-grandmother and see her whole body shaking as her eyes empty themselves and she covers her mouth with her hand.

Two

After the performance, everyone stands, the seats fold into the floor, and people collect into groups of families and friends greeting each other with hugs, kisses, more tears, and held hands as the many domes of the *Euclid* empty out. The volunteer Ceremony Planning Committee, composed of people from all vocations—Research, Services, Operations—has encouraged everyone to gather in the Deck One Park, the largest of the *Euclid*'s arboretums. It's equipped with its own dome that converts from opaque to transparent, to let in starlight. One of the few places on the ship large enough to accommodate the forty thousand colonists aboard.

As we leave the dome and walk down the now bright and blue-skied corridor toward a less-crowded maglev station than the one just outside the dome, my parents, aunts, and uncles argue the details of a group dinner tonight, determined to not let family fall by the wayside in the midst of the crowds and chaotic celebration. I walk with my great-grandmother, who stays a few paces back from the cluster, content to let her grandchildren work out the details. As one of the oldest people aboard, she enjoys the freedom of retirement and has few obligations, volunteering as a gardener in the parks and visiting Prime School history classes to tell the younger kids stories from a hundred years ago. Whatever time people pick for dinner will be fine with her. I give her my arm to hold onto.

"How does it feel?" I ask her. Her grandchildren have been worrying for the last ten years that she might not live to see orbit.

"I'm rejoicing," she says, her wide smile deepening every crevice of her face. "I never expected it, you know."

I blush a little at her bluntness. "That sounds so sad."

"I never worried about it," she says. "When I was in Path School, my parents made clear I was born thirty years too early to see it. Knowing you'd be around would have to be enough. It sounds horrid, but understand— my grandparents, especially my mother's father, were very bitter. The older he got, the more he complained."

Sometimes at the largest family gatherings, I see her sitting by herself, watching children like me as if we are from some different ship. Or maybe we're exactly the way she was eighty years ago.

She imitates her grandfather's scowl: "He used to say, 'Not just me, but everyone I know will be dead before we get there. All we get is a supposedly comfortable ship.' He was almost right, and it was too much for my grandmother. She left him when she was sixty. When you and your cousins were born, I could say to myself, 'I've lived long enough to know someone who will see it.' I made sure my own children knew this, too. Made sure they were grateful."

Her eyes wander as she turns over the old memories like soil in one of her garden plots. "My grandfather came from such an unhappy family. My parents tried to be more optimistic, but they weren't. I decided I was going to break that chain. People on this ship have a long and cherished history of caring for one another and working through conflicts together, and I was not going to let my family be the exception."

Her grandfather would have been only two or three generations removed from Midflight, what my history teacher calls the *Euclid*'s moment of truth, a time of shipwide disagreement that nearly resulted in a colony schism.

The Helena Orbit

Naomi Delerue, a pioneer in telescope spectrometry, looked through her data one day and declared that Helena not only held an atmosphere of mostly carbon dioxide and argon but that it also appeared to have life. Still a good two-hundred and fifty years out, many of the colonists decided that the risk of either uninhabitability or high-order complex life, which would render colonization impossible or unethical, was too great to justify the remainder of the trip.

They attempted to convince the rest of the colony to either turn around and return to Earth or find a better planet to colonize. The disagreements escalated, and in the end a referendum showed that only a quarter of the colonists supported changing destination, a decision which could render the lives and toil of the previous two-hundred fifty years wasted. Alternative planets were sought out anyway, and every effort was made to accommodate the needs of the dissatisfied faction, but it took years of negotiation between groups and many more referendums to quell their discontent.

Even now, the details of dinner decided, my mother returns to her fear that this reception will spur nothing but ethical debates about bioengineering and colonization, with people forgetting to savor this truly singular moment of arrival.

"You have too little faith in people," my father says, a few paces in front of me. This has been his response at each of the times my mother has voiced similar complaints at the dinner table for the past few weeks. He says, "People know how to be happy and look beyond their differences for a day."

"Not on this ship," she says. My parents refuse to support any terraforming efforts which wipe out Helena's extant ecosystem, regardless of whether it's low-complexity, and they support the genetic modification of human beings to survive as an equal, competing part of such a system, no matter how extensive such modifications might have to be.

I shake my head at the conversation, and walk with Great-grandma in silence. We enter the maglev station. I pat her hand as it rests in the crook of my elbow. I tend to take my father's side, believing people can overcome differences, but Great-grandma's sheer contentment makes the whole argument feel nonsensical. There's a saying among astrophysicists: all stars burn out someday.

Mom leans on Dad as we wait for the maglev pods, and they hold each other at the waist.

Even they can't forget the day's joy for very long.

More than anything else at this event, I plan to look for Haruko and tell her how incredible her symphony was, but forty thousand others likely plan the same thing, so I may not get the chance until we see each other in school tomorrow.

My family and I ride the pods to the park, whose trees, fields, paths, and hills now fill with people, and whose high and currently transparent ceiling lets in the bright surface of Helena above us. Colonists stand talking in groups under the trees, sit eating on chairs they've programmed into their portable marbles, and stroll smiling along the paths.

Roaming cylindrical food dispensers slide their waist-high chassis aside to let colonists by, and these friendly AIs offer meal suggestions to those who approach. A few Path School musicians I recognize from Choir have set up a band shell and dance floor near one of the park's walls, where they play centuries-old jazz standards mixed with original songs. One member sits playing a keyboard instrument of her own invention wherein the vibrations pass through water before echoing in resonance chambers similar to organ pipes.

Usually, the whole colony gathers only on the first of the month for any referendums, and does so in the bleak Assembly Hall that spans sections of decks twelve to fourteen and offers no window into space. A colony-wide reception of eating and mingling happens on other holidays like Launch Day, but attendance is never anywhere near the whole. This time, the reception will continue long enough for everyone to attend, even the Operations Crew, who need to do so in shifts.

The Helena Orbit

My family, having finalized dinner plans, has now gone its separate ways, so I open my marble into a network portal to see if Haruko is nearby. The ship's network tells me that her locater's been set on Private.

I try to call her through the marble. Had the performance taken that much out of her?

"She is not taking calls," the network tells me.

Has she checked into the medical deck?

No answer available.

I pace around the grass. Haruko had had enough recent trips to the medical deck that I know her usual doctors, so I ask the network to locate each of them. Most are here in the park. One had a shift start right after the ceremony, and is now working. Not taking calls. As a last-ditch effort, I call Haruko's parents. Her mother picks up.

"Hi, Mrs. K. This is Edwyn Santiago. Do you know where Haruko is? Is she OK?"

"She's here. We're on the hospital deck, in Con-Ob. She's all right. Not really up for visitors."

Con-Ob meant constant observation. Haruko's condition, which arose mysteriously a month ago, has flared-up twice since then. Her doctors have posited a variety of hypotheses from the bacterial to the genetic to some combination of the two, but whatever happened mutated her skin to such an extent that the doctors believe there must be a foreign contaminant involved— maybe something she came into contact with in one of the biotech labs, given the diversity of cell growth occurring. They put their test results on the network, and a flood of possibilities has come in from various biology labs, but so far none of the projects could explain Haruko's symptoms. Since the first flare-up, Haruko's skin has shown a sickly greenish tint, and has bruised much more easily and lost some elasticity, limiting her movements. The skinsuit she wore, secreting compounds designed to keep her surfaces intact during the performance today, was only a temporary fix, like the various therapy suits she's worn to school that essentially move her body for her, preventing the most taxing motions.

"Can I talk to her? I won't be long. I promise."

"One second."

I rest my thumb on my lips as I wait, trying not to bite the nail.

"She says she'd like to hear from you. But she's weak. Just say hello, and that's really it."

I sit down in the grass. "Thank you. Thank you so much."

The network asks me to switch calls, and I allow it.

"Edwyn?"

"Haruko. Are you OK?"

"My arms feel like they're back on Io, but otherwise I'm no worse than usual."

I bite my nail. Can't help it. Then I say, "Listen, your symphony . . ." My throat catches. "I can't . . . I can still feel it. I can't even think about it for too long. It went nova."

She pauses, in that way artists do when they can't quite accept they've succeeded. "Thank you."

The music from the band echoes over the trees. I tell her, "I feel like I could never listen to another piece."

"I feel like I could never write one."

For a second the two of us just breathe. "Thanks for talking," I say. "I'm glad you're all right."

"Thanks for calling. Say hi to everyone." Her request makes me tense inside. I hate bearing bad news. But I tell myself she'll get better. I know she will.

"I'll do that," I say.

We hang up. I close the network port back into a marble, and I pull my knees against me. Helena fills the sky like an ancient myth made manifest. All this time we've referred to the planet as "she," and imbuing it with some sense of personhood feels natural. Centuries ago, and maybe still, some people referred to their home planet as "mother Earth." Illogical yet deeply appealing. Helena, too, has given birth to life. Dense vegetation. Its oceans likely teem. All of us scientists and soon-to-be scientists turn our eyes toward that life now, thrilled at the prospect of unraveling the conundrum of complex organisms evolving without oxygen. The rest of us go about our lives unable to shake from our minds the question of whether we can call this planet home. The next few days will give us universes of data, but science, like a beheaded hydra, throws back more questions from every answer we wrest.

A well-meaning food dispenser hums up next to me, but I wave it away. I check the time on the network. Two hours until family dinner. I stand up, brush the grass from my dress, and walk down the path toward a grove where some friends of mine and Haruko's agreed to meet up. Everyone I pass gives a smile and nod, and I return it. Maybe our hopes will be justified.

#

Hesper and Isaac sit under a tree on chairs they've programmed into their marbles. Hesper wears an early-*Euclid* formal dress, flowing and iridescent with uncountable pieces sewn together. Intricacy typical of the creative boom that characterized the first few generations of colonists, who saw their ship more as a home that happened to be moving through space, a place for people to simply live and create, rather than worrying about destinations. They were happy, the records say, because they chose to leave Io behind. They were where they wanted to be. Hesper's hair, short, bright, and all curls, looks equally intricate, as always, but the dress brings it out.

Isaac, one-upping her historical bent, reconstructed a capitalist-era tuxedo from images in the archives, programming it into his clothes marble piece by piece from specifications found in obscure files almost unreadable by collaborative-era technology. His nearly shaved head completes the simple neatness of the look, and he's even reprogrammed his ergotread shoes to look like shined leather.

When Isaac sees me, he runs to give me a hug, and Hesper follows, more restrained. "You're not acting the part," she says after him, smiling. "People in tuxedos tried to show they were 'rich' and 'respectable.'"

"I'm not in a play," he says back to her while he hugs me. He lets go and faces her again. "And besides, even kids used to rent them to go to school dances. It wasn't just for the ruling class."

"Can we take a break from history?" I say. "I've had about all I can take for one day. Speaking of which, Haruko says hi."

Hesper leans close and we pat each other on the back, not quite hugging. Hesper likes her space. "How is Haruko?" she asks. "I haven't seen her anywhere."

"Hospital. She's a little beat up from conducting."

"Burning Io," Isaac says. "Those doctors have to do better."

I say, "You two see anything through the scopes last night?"

Hesper sweeps her dress close to her legs and sits back down in her chair. "Mountains and clouds and what look like forests. Same old. You should do marine bio with me."

"I'll think about it. Speaking of that, I met an interesting first-year apprentice this morning."

Isaac looks up from scrolling through his marble's programs and says, "Details!"

I laugh. "His name's Rio. He's in geology."

"Heavens around," says Hesper. "Geology? The first extraterrestrial bio ever discovered, looking us in the face, and he'd rather map tectonic plates?"

"He does his own thing. That was part of what made him interesting. He said I should consider choosing a mentor who gets me excited about my work instead of just doing what I'm best at."

Isaac sidles up to me. "And are you excited about geology now? It gets your rocks moving?"

Hesper snorts, waving over a food dispenser.

I push Isaac away. "I don't have rocks," I say. "Whatever that means. I haven't found anything I'm excited about yet. And there are already so many Pathers applying for marine bio mentors. My mom wants me to do bioengineering or synth-bio."

Now holding a cup of tea on her lap, Hesper raises her eyebrows. "And not even study the planet at all?"

I pull out my marble and flip through the chair programs. "I don't know. She's convinced I'd be like Mozart or something. And I'd get to use the findings from the planet, just not for a couple of years. Somebody's got to use the data and not just make more discoveries." I find a large cushion program, choose it, and sit down.

"If you don't decide soon, you might get stuck there," Isaac says. "Those discovery spots are already almost filled. There'll be hardly anybody at the Expo except for those development fields."

"I know; I'm bringing it on myself. But I like Rio's idea. There's so much to choose from, even just in development, that I'm bound to find a mentor I like somewhere." Hesper and Isaac knew what they wanted to research in their second year of Path, and applied early. I focused instead on excelling in general, which my dad told me would help bring a more creative mind to whatever I did end up picking. I'm not sorry I listened to him.

The food dispenser slides over to me and this time I indulge it, choosing a black bean salad. In Prime School the teachers always encouraged us to sample the food staples of our genetic heritage, but much of the cuisine I've found too spicy. I've traced my genes all the way back to ancestors in the Earth nation of Mexico, but that was more interesting to me as an illustration of the gene-pool algorithms that select for maintaining diversity in the population than it was as some kind of addition to my identity—though I did discover flamenco music this way, and that's stayed on my studying playlist.

Still, as far as genetic heritage goes, I'm more interested in why my bio parents applied to have a child two hundred years after their deaths. They were part of a subculture that appealed to save their sperm and eggs to have children born who would be able to see the *Euclid* end her journey. Was life two hundred years ago so terrible? I've heard of one or two others whose bio-parents did the same thing, though we're rare enough I've never taken the time to meet any of them.

But nobody's raised by their bio parents anymore, and I think I'm much more like my mom and dad than I'm like the two people who had their sperm and eggs archived for two centuries.

"You can always apply to go into Operations," Hesper says. "If you need some extreme hierarchy in your life."

I laugh. "That just became the most boring vocation on board. What are they going to do besides maintain orbit and replace old parts? I'd sooner go into Service and sit on a referendum committee."

"Mark my words," says Isaac. "The next Artist Laureate will be a former ref-com sitter. My dads come home and immediately start drawing or programming something."

"I like it," Hesper says. "I hope they all do that, after carrying the weight of forty thousand opinions on their shoulders."

"Why don't you find your new crush and say hi?" Isaac says to me.

"He's not a crush. I just said he was interesting."

"Difference being?"

"The extent of interest."

"You're blushing!"

"I have idiopathic craniofacial erythema."

"And I'm a secret clone manufactured from the recombined-matter dispenser!"

Hesper bursts out laughing and rocks back in her chair.

I hide my cheeks with my hands. "Don't make fun. Dignity."

Isaac pats me on the back. "I won't tell, I promise."

I hold the edges of my food dish and take a long, counselor-recommended breath to calm myself down. "We should raise the research age until adolescent emotions subside. Scientists shouldn't have crushes."

"And take all the fun out of it?" Isaac says. "What for? Besides, I'm not convinced they ever subside."

"That's for sure," Hesper says. "I can just see that referendum curling up and dying."

Isaac pulls up the network on his screen. "Latest bulletin: Future bioengineer diagnosed with love at first sight. Objectivity of lab results questioned."

I can't help a smile. "Okay, can we talk about something else?"

"Check out the latest imaging of Helena's oceans," Hesper says. She puts her teacup in the grass and stands up, then collapses her chair and stretches it into a monitor as tall as she is. "This came in yesterday." She explains shaded areas on a map of the planet, pointing out locations of suspected reefs and likely areas of high-density marine populations. Data all expected to be confirmed or refined within the next few days.

"We know you're excited," Isaac says. "You don't have to bore us, too."

"Hey. Dignity."

"I'm joking! Why is everybody playing the dignity card?"

I finish eating and put the dish into the food dispenser's intake slot. "How about a real game? With actual cards? Any takers?"

"I'm in," Isaac says. "I've even got a prop!" He takes a deck of Earth playing cards from the pocket of his tuxedo. "I'm still learning to shuffle, though."

"More history?" Hesper says. "Why not use a Jupiter deck? I want to play Alignment."

"We can do that! Numbered cards can be resources and face cards are the moons. Aces are the big red spot. Io is the joker."

Hesper rolls her eyes. "We'd need an hour to agree on the house rules."

"What about Pegasus?" I say. "That's pretty close to Rummy."

Hesper considers it. "That'll work."

Isaac pockets the deck and morphs his network monitor into a low card table. "Play to five hundred?"

Hesper nods. "Collaborative or competitive?"

Isaac grimaces. "It's a holiday, remember? Let loose. Winner takes all of the imaginary points."

Hesper looks at me. "He's a capitalist, I'm telling you."

I smile. "Careful, you'll get him in trouble."

He deals the cards.

Around us, people pass, all smiling. By turns this park may see every colonist aboard in the next twelve hours. Even Haruko, if her doctors can mend her well enough. I keep an eye out for familiar faces.

Sometimes, when I feel like doing nothing, I surf the network and land at random profiles, just to discover a name or face I haven't seen. To see what breakthroughs lie on the verge, what evolution our ship and society are seeing, what character we have as a people.

I have yet to overhear any debates about colonization today. My father, a counselor and member of the intra-colony social planning committee, has his finger on the psychological pulse of the population. So far, he's been right that today people prefer to celebrate.

My mother, a member of that same committee and many others, does what Isaac's parents do: talk through proposed referendums all day with other colonists, following the constitutional guidelines that determine whether a proposal is put out for the population to vote on. She sits between young idealists half her age and wizened veterans from her parents' generation, and under the eye of the public and the press, they consider and debate, bring in experts, run simulations, and make our society what it is. I've watched her on the network, seen her gesture with each word as she lays down her position with a certainty brought forth by the late nights she stays up poring over research publications on the network and notating points for her presentations. At the committee table, people fall into a deeply respectful silence, aware that whether they agree with her conclusions or not, her words will always warrant consideration.

My father, only occasionally at the same table as she, lets her words enter him through closed eyes as he rests his chin on his thick clasped hands. He does not do the painstaking reading she does, but instead brings anecdotal evidence from his counseling, in his deep, soft voice. He prefaces his comment with words like: "Consider this story I heard from a troubled colonist." Sometimes it supports what my mother says, and sometimes it doesn't. Once, when I was still in Prime School, he ended his story with a statement directed solely at my mother: "Your point of view, while logically sound, ignores the emotional needs of many."

She didn't speak to him for days afterward, fuming, mulling over his words, and sitting at her home workstation with dozens of research files open at once. Having learned how to resolve conflicts collaboratively in Prime School, I approached my mother often during her silence, parroting lessons about working together to find the roots of the problem and about searching for a solution to meet the needs of both parties.

"I've heard enough about meeting needs to last me as long as I live," she said. I left her alone, ready to cry at her disregard for me and for everything I had learned about the way society was supposed to work, still too young then to see the doggedness that the ideals I learned in school required in practice.

Finally, she emerged from her study one evening at dinner, sat down, looked my father in the eye, and said, evenly, "You're right. I wasted effort on that proposal. But something had to be said."

"It did," he said. "And you said it well."

They sat with their hands on their thighs, leaving me the only one touching the food.

"Next time you disagree, tell me ahead of the broadcast," she said to him. "Please."

"I'm sorry," he said. "It only came to me as I listened."

"Then maybe we shouldn't be on the same committee."

"Perhaps not."

Even at twelve, I knew his tone on those last words belied them and revealed that he couldn't give up his voice in the process of lawmaking any more than she could. They both stayed on. But never again did my father voice a concern she wasn't prepared for, and I don't recall any other time she wouldn't speak to him. Only when I got old enough for Path School could I bring to mind the memory of their tension and see that what looked at the time like complete irreverence for our colony's precepts was in fact the simple and everyday difficulty of upholding those very dictums. We were all human, and following the laws necessitated the occasional frustration.

The evening after that awkward dinner, they sat on a love seat and watched a performance on the network, falling asleep leaning on each other like they hadn't just come through their own miniature version of Midflight. How could they pretend things hadn't been terrible earlier that day? I went into my sphere that night and sat among the stars, unable to resolve the apparent contradiction. Six years later, I look to my parents as models of the partnered life.

Which isn't to say they're perfect. When I eventually get up from the card game, say goodbye to Hesper and Isaac, and go to have dinner with my family, I can't keep potential scenarios from playing out in my head as I follow the flagstone path. My aunt and uncle, who strongly believe that whatever life we find on the planet below won't be complex enough to make colonization or even terraforming unethical, won't be able to stop themselves from making some hopeful comment about living on the planet, and my mother will respond with a prediction of how many years it will take to firmly establish that no such complexity exists, and that if people don't want to live in a bubble colony isolated from the rest of the biosphere, the human body will need major modifications.

And so on it will go, hopeful versus skeptical, presumptuous versus curmudgeonly, and all of the other words they'll use to describe each other's viewpoints. I plan to sit next to Great-grandma or one of my cousins and pay the debate as little attention as possible.

The Helena Orbit

But seated around a table on a platform perched among the treetops for privacy, my relatives limit the discussion, oddly, to topics on which everyone agrees: the beauty of Haruko's symphony, the excitement of impending discoveries, the indescribable weight that feels lifted now that the *Euclid* has arrived at Helena.

Both sets of grandparents take turns reminiscing about the various notable events they've lived to witness, and I talk with my cousins about Path School and their choices of occupation. Two of my four cousins, a year behind me in Path, will go into Research and Development, like me; one, graduating at the same time as I am, chose to go into Service, like my parents; and one went into Operations a year ago just so she could be on the crew and play some part in physically bringing the *Euclid* into orbit.

Much more quickly than I expect, the meal comes to a close, and my various family clusters hug and kiss and once again go their separate ways.

I walk home with my parents, arms linked with theirs, giggling while I talk, about to collapse after the day-long celebration and excited for the Expo after a shorter day at school tomorrow. When we get home, I hug them goodnight, change to pajamas, and program my marble into a mattress within a dome. I climb in and curl up under the starfield. Helena hangs above me, still remaining, more than anything else, a question. I drift to sleep looking up at her red and purple mountain ranges, her clouded archipelagos, her colorless seas.

Three

The morning I spend in school calculating the lowest speed necessary for the *Euclid* to keep her orbit from decaying given the size, weight, and altitude of the ship and the strength of Helena's gravity well. All of us students sit scattered on knee-high ergo-cushions, working at flat screens mounted to the cushions, which can slide quickly across the floor with a gentle push. The ceiling is set on a projection of Helena's system, with her star 51 Pegasi in the center and Helena about two-thirds of the way to the wall. The other planets, all gaseous, circle closer to or further from the central sun.

Miss Young, a dark woman with a multitude of tiny braids down to her waist, makes her rounds, checking our figures. We've used all the necessary math tools before, but not in this combination, and I spend the first minute or two jotting down the order of operations and formulas onto my work screen's blank space before I even think about applying them to the provided figures. Isaac, not far from me, has already got the steps down and sits plugging numbers in faster than I can keep up. The first person to finish, if requested, has to assist the person farthest behind, and it's not uncommon for Isaac to do the assisting.

Hesper, on the other hand, looks like she hasn't moved at all, simply visualizing the problem in her head, and I've seen this result in incredibly fast work. After a couple revisions to my order, I put the numbers in and see what happens, checking my calculations each step of the way. Isaac's hands zip about his screen, nearly finished. A few seconds before him, Hesper stands up, and Miss Young comes over to check her answer. Isaac finishes next, followed by two other astrophysics-destined prodigies. It's not unheard of for an astrophysicist to later leave R&D for Ops, and even go on to become the *Euclid*'s captain. I could see Isaac getting bored with research someday, and applying for a change of vocation. Hesper, however, will likely keep studying marine bio for the rest of her life, and her insights into all kinds of problems like this one will make the rest of her job easier.

I finish the problem now, standing up with a few others, pretty par for the course when it comes to astrophysics: not my strongest suit, but nothing overwhelming, either. Miss Young comes over, almost gliding the way she does in her floor-length gray skirt. She looks at my work, and says, "Fine job, Edwyn. I like your process." She smiles, and goes on to the next student. Most of the class now stands, and the few remaining students who work on the problem have not requested assistance. Usually a good sign. Miss Young sits at her workstation and sends a new problem to the screens of those who've finished. This one is substantially more difficult, and already students are signaling their desire to form a group, and kicking the floor to slide their seats together. I take my time working out what I can before I push off and join a group myself. Miss Young places herself in the center of the room to observe our discussions.

#

At lunch, I sit with Isaac and Hesper at a table in the cafeteria. Bright windows let in sunlight from Earth's city of Hong Kong, a new simulation that has the younger Prime-schoolers crowding by the windows for a better look. Lunch, the one time we get to eat real food grown in the ship's gardens instead of recombined from bulk waste matter, always gets us into good spirits. I hold in my hands a portobello mushroom baked with olive oil and balsamic vinegar, topped with tomatoes, greens, and basil pesto, and I take a long smell before the first bite.

"If I could eat here every meal," I say, "I might go into Services."

"They do have the good life in some ways," Isaac says. "How about that second problem in Astrophysics?"

"I don't even want to talk about it," Hesper says. "Guest problem, clearly."

"We'll see," Isaac says. He's met many of the scientists in the field, and would be likely to recognize an unsolved problem from someone's research. "I thought we gave it a good shot, though."

"I guess nobody's ready to skip the apprentice stage," Hesper says. "Unless we network tonight and come back with the solution tomorrow."

"We were all missing the same piece," I said. "Did you notice that?"

A couple of Prime kids run past, a girl with a handheld gene sequencer chasing a boy.

"The algorithm doesn't lie!" she says. "You said you'd kiss me if our sequences were compatible!"

"I did not!"

A teacher stands up and walks after them. "Dignity, children. Show dignity, now."

Hesper laughs and looks at me. "You remember when we were in Human Reproduction?"

"Don't remind me," Isaac says.

"I still remember your face," I say, "when the teacher started talking about the sperm laws."

"Burning Io." Isaac counts on his fingers. "Vasectomies, sperm donation, and male pregnancy in a single lesson. Who thought that was a good idea?"

"You knew, though," Hesper says.

"Most of us knew," Isaac says. "But it's still awkward. And there was one kid whose parents decided to let the teachers break it to him. He had no idea."

"At twelve?" Hesper says. "Hadn't he heard from anybody else?"

"Weird stuff happens sometimes. Oh, and speaking of reproduction." He pulls out his marble and makes it a network screen. "I saw this earlier today." He hands it to Hesper. She looks at it and turns pale.

"I'm a mother! How am I a mother?"

Isaac shrugs. "Somebody got one of your eggs. It happens."

"And the father is . . . heavens around, not Dr. Calypso!" Hesper leans back and slumps in her chair. "He's practically my parents' age!"

I try to keep a laugh in and fail. "At least you never have to meet the kid."

"Have you met me? Of course I have to meet the kid."

I reach for the screen and she hands it to me. "Who's having it?" I say.

"A group I don't know. They live in Lower Stern. Two men and three women."

"Plenty of parents to go around, anyway," I say. "Oh. Plenty of siblings, too."

"Having more than two parents isn't all it's cracked up to be," Hesper says. She has four, an equal mix of sexes, and after eighteen years has come to the conclusion that they're all just friends and aren't actually partnered. I have my doubts.

"Lower Stern is where Rio lives," I say.

Hesper grabs the screen back from me. "Okay, I need some dust on this guy," she says.

"I don't want to look him up," I say, my face hot.

Hesper frowns at the screen. "Hmm. 'Him' might not be the right pronoun."

"You're kidding me!" I grab the screen back and look at Rio's profile. It's Rio, all right, but the sex is listed as neither M nor F nor any of the other usual variations. Instead, it's X. "I could have sworn Rio was male," I say. "I guess I was presumptuous. But everybody and their cousin has a Z chromosome. This is something else, right?" I think back to my health classes on human gender variation, trying to remember all the possibilities.

"I've met a few Xs," Isaac says. "Mostly friends of both my dads. One transitioned to female and then changed her profile to F. Another presented as androgynous. Not too rare, really."

I look through the rest of Rio's profile. The pronoun set Rio uses is Khe, a set that isn't neutral but specifically third-gender. Khe completed Prime School last year, appropriate for a first-year apprentice. On a whim, I look at the research interests listed. Plate tectonics, naturally, planet formation and composition, and bingo, intersex conditions. Born somewhere in between male and female from the start.

"I guess this could be it," I say, and hand it to Isaac.

"Makes sense," he says. "I wonder how the reproduction laws apply."

"There's a clause for it somewhere," I say. "I remember my mom citing it in one of her proposals a while back."

Isaac hands it to Hesper. She glances at it and hands it back to me with a shrug. "Well," she says. "You said khe was interesting."

I close the profile. Yes, I had thought Rio interesting, but now I picture khes face and it looks completely different, because now I've learned—or I assume— another sliver of what's beneath it. The attraction I had felt doesn't diminish: gender had never mattered much in that. Instead, as crushes tended to, the attraction intensified slightly with every new piece of information, regardless of content. I wondered how quickly I could fall for someone I didn't quite know, and how foolish that might be.

"Thinking deep thoughts?" Hesper says.

"I wish," I say. "Mostly questions."

"That's a good scientist." Isaac pats me on the back.

After lunch, I part ways with Hesper and Isaac, and swim up a zerograv chute to the next deck for my biotech lecture. It's a gym lecture, so we tap our waistband keypads and change from our white lab skinsuits into sweat-wicking ones before getting onto the treadmills that circle the teacher. Each treadmill has a screen large enough to give minute details on the tech specs we're learning today. We run and we read along with the lecture. Two hundred years ago, most of the *Euclid*'s computers used manufactured DNA to store data, and today's lecture traces the evolution of those designs into the mostly polymer but partially organic marbles we all carry and into which we program furniture and devices. Everything, including the *Euclid*'s central network hub, still uses DNA data storage. Much of this I've learned already, having a mother who studies biotech and biotech law every day, but the class goes quickly.

When it ends, we line up to fill our water bottles from the wall dispenser on the way out, and in the corridor I find Haruko waiting for me. Thankful for the sweatsuit that keeps me sanitary, I give her a long hug. "I was worried."

"I'm fine."

I take a look at her. I can't help associating the green of her skin with mold and rot and other horrors, but her skin also has taken a kind of reflective tint underneath that. Still green, but metallic, as if she has a layer of aluminum leafing under her skin. She can't wear a programmable outfit like most people because her condition requires specially medicating materials. It's covered with little diagnostic readouts, and makes me remember the days, so recent, when she could design outfits she enjoyed. Before her daily life changed completely.

"Any progress?"

"They're narrowing down the causes and possibilities to only a few, but they have a ways to go. No more conducting for a while."

"You're probably fine with that."

"More than fine. I have the rest of the week off. Medical leave."

"Nice. Want to walk with me?"

We go down the corridor toward the Expo, which I've been trying to avoid thinking about. It runs for a day and a half, and if I haven't applied for at least three apprenticeships by the time it ends, the computer will match my skills to whatever positions remain open. Still hot and breathing hard from my run, I drink my water. The sky in the corridor grays with clouds, making the air feel cooler.

"You've probably had nonstop congratulations," I say.

"It's odd," she says. "It's great on the one hand, but in the back of my mind I'm already worrying about having nothing else to work on. At least now I have time to listen to what the rest of the ship is doing, and see people again."

"Want to crash the Expo?"

She laughs. "I might. It's been too long since I did some science."

"It's been too long since I did some music."

"How's Choir?"

"It's fine. Hasn't been as much fun since we started singing post-Midflight pieces."

"You sound like Hesper."

"It's true though. I feel like the ship stopped believing in muses or something. Present company excluded."

"I just believe in the collective unconscious."

"It's enough." I shake my head, uncomfortable with my sudden rush of negativity. "I really don't want to do biotech," I say. "Or bioengineering. Or bio-anything."

"Excellent. You have the beginning of a very clear vision."

"One my mom won't like."

"Well, if I may share an observation," Haruko clasps her hands behind her back, a little uncomfortably, "your parents interpret the conflict resolution laws as conflict avoidance laws. No offense to their dignity. They're great people."

"That's the problem."

We round a corner and find ourselves in the exhibit hall, a maze of presenters and projections, demonstrations of experiments, and recruiters looking to match you with your perfect apprenticeship. Data screens loom everywhere, backdropping the various presenters with graphics related to their research. A recruiter comes up to us, a man who towers over me and Haruko with a welcoming grin. He wears the uniform of an Ops crew member.

"How are you young ladies?" he says. "I'm Lieutenant Ferguson from the propulsion quarter." After a second he recognizes Haruko. "Pleasure to meet you, Miss Kanno," he says. He doesn't acknowledge her sickly green, metallic skin. He doesn't realize how serious it is.

She smiles. "Thanks for getting us into orbit."

"You're absolutely welcome. And you should know that Operations is always looking for new people." He looks from her to me. "So if you can't find anything that matches your skills the way you'd prefer, you can always apply for a vocation change."

"I'll keep that in mind," I say. "For right now, I'd like to see some of the demos. But I'll come back if I have any questions."

"I'll be here," he says.

We walk into the crowd. "Ops is looking desperate," I say.

"Struggling for relevance. But they're never too far short of their recruitment goals. I know people who crave that kind of structure. One of the artist Laureates a few generations back used to do portraits of the Ops crew. It's not as boring as it sounds."

"All of these demos look great," I say, distracted. "But how am I supposed to know what I'll be into?"

"Stop theorizing," Haruko says. "Find a project you can't keep yourself away from."

"That's similar to what an interesting boy—um, person, told me yesterday. Khe's probably here somewhere, actually."

"What's this person do?"

"Geology."

"Any appeal there?"

I don't meet her eyes. "Not from the field, no."

"But you'll want to visit the demo anyway."

"I might."

We walk a little further. Images of Helena or various sections of her are everywhere.

"Do something unexpected," Haruko says. "Go somewhere you never imagined yourself."

"Like what?"

"Look around. What do you know next to nothing about?" Haruko faces this way and that, reading off the various fields nearby. "Propulsion? Prosthetics? Botanical ecosystems? Let's go."

The prosthetic leg the young researcher demonstrates looks completely real and biological, and halfway through her showing us its design process using DNA donated from a volunteer, I lean toward Haruko and say, "This is biotech. I understand every word she's telling us, even though I've never set foot in her lab. I could even tell you the problems she's likely to explain next."

Haruko smiles. "And none of it interests you. Off we go. But you do realize this is your talent."

"I've spent the last four years excelling at this stuff. I'm ready for something new."

"You're insatiable."

"I can't help it! None of the problems in the field are ones I care about."

"I know. Check out propulsion."

A huge screen shows a diagram of a proposed system to boost the already nearly perfect efficiency of the ship's fuel cells, by redesigning the whole thing and throwing out the five-hundred-year-old models that did with unparalleled persistence exactly what they were built for. Getting their first rest now since the beginning of the fifty-year deceleration burn, they only burst occasionally to prevent orbital decay. If there's a time to build new ones and scrap the old, it's now. But it saddens me. Have I gotten sentimental about the ship's design?

"Not resonating with me."

"I'm not surprised. Mechanical engineering was never your favorite."

We tread on toward the botanical ecosystems platform, but halfway there I notice what lies between us and it: geology.

"Help me out," I say to Haruko. I grab her hand and steer us toward the booth, where Rio sits behind a table, next to a globe of Helena as tall as khe is. It's been intricately mapped, and a large wedge cut out of it shows the planet's interior structure, as it's currently understood.

"Hi there," I say. Rio stands up. I don't let khen speak yet. "You should have told me you'd be here."

Khe looks back and forth from me to Haruko, still appearing fully male as far as I can tell, and as attractively so as ever. So much for deep questions.

"I assumed you'd assume I would be," Rio says, and smiles. "Poor communication, obviously. But you also didn't show any interest in the field, that I noticed." I do spy a kind of impossible smoothness to khes face, like maybe khe never shaves. But khes overly formal tone throws me back a bit, so different from the casual way khe spoke to me yesterday. Rio turns to Haruko. "Miss Kanno," khe says, extending a hand. "Pleasure to see you again. I hope you're on your way to recovery. Congratulations on your symphony."

She shakes khes hand. "Did you like the counterpoint?"

"I tried not to focus inordinately on it. But yes. Beautifully done."

I let go of Haruko's other hand, reflexively, but smile. "I didn't realize you two had met."

"Indeed," Haruko says. "I thought you might have meant Rio when you mentioned geology. We met last year, before Rio graduated. When I learned more about khen, I later decided to symbolize gender and sex variance with one iteration in the third movement, using a lot of perfect thirds in that particular permutation of the melody."

How much history do they have? I say, "So how do you . . . categorize yourself, if that's not too personal?"

Khe shrugs. "Just intersex. If you mean the medical aspect, it's congenital adrenal hyperplasia due to 21 hydroxylase deficiency."

I blink, thinking. "The algorithm doesn't select that out?"

Khe smiles. "Am I incapable of a dignified life?"

"No! No, I didn't mean it like that! Wow, sorry, no. I just thought . . . it sounded like a . . . like it might show up only in much smaller populations. I'm wrong. I'm sorry."

No hint of a smile now, and khes words remain coldly clinical. "My parents had chances during the pregnancy to ensure gonadal development aligned with my chromosomes, but saw no ethical requirement to do so. The adrenal issues have been addressed. I haven't suffered."

"Except from my stupidity. Sorry." Did my brain take a day off? Scientists definitely shouldn't have crushes. "So tell me about this model of Helena."

Khe follows my lead to change the subject, steps back, and points to the cutout portion showing the planet's insides. "We've taken enough readings to be reasonably sure that the lithosphere operates in much the same way as Earth's, allowing for seafloor spreading and continental drifts. Not a surprise by any means, but it helps us to be more certain when mapping the tectonic plates. We're still several hundred quakes and volcanic eruptions away from a complete map of the plates' movements, but every day we're learning something new." Khe pivots the model around and points to a small continent near the southern magnetic pole. "This area has shown volcanic activity unusually high compared to most of the other plates, so figuring out the reasons for this is among our top priorities."

So achingly formal. What effect does Haruko have on khen? I say, "So that's what's under those clouds. I've seen maps that showed mountains, but your model is better."

Khe smiles, but says nothing.

"Oh, you are modest today," Haruko says. "Rio built that model khenself. By hand."

"Wait, you didn't print this?"

Khe still beams. "No. I projected topo maps onto the surface and sculpted based on those."

"Khe's been working on it for a year, refining it every time we got new data."

"Please, Miss Kanno. You sensationalize."

"What do you think, Edwyn? Geology your thing?"

"It looks interesting," I say. "But I want to keep looking."

Rio puts khes arm out as if to usher us onward. "By all means."

I stride quickly across the showroom floor with Haruko in tow. "What just happened?"

"What do you mean?"

"Were you two involved?"

"Not really. Khe fell for me pretty hard about a year ago, but I wasn't interested. Partly the timing, partly just the barest bit too logical to be my type."

"Is khe still . . . after you?"

"We're amicable. Rio knows it's not going to happen. And ever since I was named Laureate, khe's been super formal. It's khes way of showing me khe would rather keep me at a distance. That's my interpretation, anyway."

I look at the floor as we cross the exhibit hall. "Now I feel even stupider."

"You were ridiculously cute tripping over yourself like that."

"Don't make fun."

"I'm not. I think khe found it endearing."

"Endearing that I wondered why khe was allowed to be born? I know my genetic conditions better than that. I looked like an idiot."

"Dignity. You did not. I'm sure khe could tell you were nervous."

"That makes me feel light years better."

We reach the botanical ecosystems platform. A network screen shows a flat map of Helena's two largest continents, which are heavily forested by complex plants that shouldn't exist in the mostly carbon dioxide atmosphere. An older woman in a turtleneck and an old-fashioned lab coat sits on a spindly chair with her hands in her pockets, watching the passers-by. She waves at us as we approach.

"Looking for a field?" she says.

"That's me," I say.

She stands from the chair and steps down from the platform. "Great place to be. What's your background?"

"Biotech. But I don't really like it." Something about her manner, the crow's feet and happy wrinkles around her mouth, instantly disarms me.

"Well, we can't have that," she pats me on the back. "What are you looking for?"

"I don't know. Something I can get excited about."

"Well, my dear, you just arrived at the most underrated platform at the whole expo. Let me show you what I do."

She pulls a marble from her pocket, turns it into a control panel, and manipulates the map on the platform's big screen. "The vegetation on Helena's two largest continents isn't nearly as diverse as we were expecting. So far we've only identified a few hundred species of plant life, when we were expecting a hundred thousand. After all, if one form of complex life can evolve without oxygen, why not a million forms?"

"But you don't work on figuring out how the plants evolved without oxygen?"

"Nope. That's the evolutionary bio platform over there, the microbio platform over there, and the marine bio platform way over there. And that's why they draw the crowds. Everybody knows that what those fields discover will potentially upend a lot of the Earth-based biology we've taken for granted. So if that's the question that gets you excited, please. Go fall in line with the other applicants."

"You two have fun," Haruko says. "I'll catch up with you later, all right?"

I wave absently, absorbed in the conversation. I say, "It sounds too intense, to be honest. I like to observe things more than I like to dissect things."

She leans close to me and whispers. "And that's the irony! They don't even get to dissect! They all think people will be setting foot on this planet within a year, maybe. You know what's more realistic? Five. Ten years. Until we know exactly what kinds of organisms are down there, and how they might interact with all the organisms up here, nobody's going anywhere close to any kind of biotic environment outside this ship. A single

47

dividing, oxygen-producing cyanobacterium could eventually wipe out the planet's entire ecology!" She laughs. "And they all know that!" She shakes her arm at the distant platforms and the crowds around them. "But they're young, so they're racing to make the first breakthrough. They think breakthroughs happen at the drop of a hat, instead of after years of dropping hats over and over and recording the results until you finally realize you should try dropping something else. The truth is, they'll be staring at computer images and digital models of these organisms for a lot longer than they think before they ever get to see one in person."

I can't help asking: "And what will we be doing?"

She pokes me gently on my chest bone. "So glad you asked. While all of them are sitting reading lists of elements in quarantined air samples taken by drones, and analyzing the structures of their single-celled organisms on flat little screens, you and I will be observing the ecosystem at work as if we were standing right there on the ground. My lab has its own simulator and a set of three imaging satellites earmarked for our use. The satellites give us our 3D feed, and we get to play in it."

"That sounds amazing."

"Well," she says. "I do exaggerate a little. Plants interact on very long time scales that most people don't have the patience for. We'll be visiting carefully selected sites every day, looking at what's different, and basically doing nothing but collecting data for the first, I don't know, two years."

"You're kidding."

"Like I said, breakthroughs take time. And patience. Nobody wants to do the same thing over and over every day, but that's what we need to do. When I get to that part, everyone leaves because they want faster results. And don't get me wrong, discoveries will be coming by the shipload every day, in every field that studies Helena. But discoveries, ultimately, are just data. Once you've made them, things taper off quickly, and everybody's in the same boat: analyze the data. Collect more data. But I can do that while seeing what it looks like to stand on the highest mountain peak or walk on the beach by the ocean. I'm limited by what the satellites can see, but that's still plenty to explore. So it's a matter of taste. And of getting used to wearing the simulator suit. And, once again, of patience."

"That sounds like fun. My mother won't know what to do with herself, though."

"Is this your career or hers?"

I shift my weight, shuffle my feet a little. "It's not hers."

"If you want to apply, apply. If not, don't. But I think we can have some fun with it."

She morphs her control panel into a network screen with an application. She hands it to me. I pull up my profile and let it fill in the fields.

"Edwyn Santiago," she says. "I've heard your name before. Don't remember where, but I take it as a good sign. My name's Pamela Portsmouth. Nice to meet you."

"Thank you for considering me," I say.

"Considering's already done. You'll get an acceptance notice in the morning."

"Are you serious?"

"Get some good sleep tonight. Think seriously about the repetition before deciding if you'll take the job."

"I will. Thank you."

She smiles. "No, thank you. I get to go home now. It's noisy in here."

I turn from the platform and head for the exit. Across the showroom I see Haruko, still here somehow. She's talking to Rio. I decide I'd rather not overhear and take a wide path around them.

Four

When I see my parents at dinner, we sit down around the table, set the walls on a colorful Earth sunset panorama, and observe a moment of silent gratitude for the community and technology which have kept us alive and fed. We savor the first bite, tonight of a pasta dish we all enjoy.

As soon as the first bite is over, my mother looks at me and says, "So do you have some big news for us?"

I look from her to my father. They are both smiling.

"I do. I spoke with a researcher at the Expo today, and she told me I'd have an acceptance notice in the morning."

My mother claps quietly. "I'm so proud, sweetie. What field? Something in bioengineering, right?"

Might as well get it over with. "Actually, no."

The silence falls instantly.

"Well, don't keep us waiting," my mother says, laughing and throwing a glance at my father, her voice nervous.

"Botanical ecosystems."

My mother can't keep the frown away. "But doing what?"

"Studying how the different plant species interact, compete, cooperate."

She puts her napkin on the table. "I don't believe this. With your credentials, you couldn't get accepted into a bio lab? That's impossible."

"I didn't apply."

My mother's face morphs to shock. "Not to any?"

51

"Mom, if I was going to do biotech or bioengineering, I would have applied early, like everyone else. Dad could have told you that."

"You're joking." She turns to my father, who has been listening with his hands on his lap.

"She means I had figured it out," he says. He turns to me. "You could have told your mother that yourself, if you had made up your mind."

"I hadn't," I say. "Not really. I would have applied if I hadn't found something else."

"As a last resort, because you knew you were good enough," my mother says. "And now what happens to all that knowledge and expertise you've built up? You won't use any of it."

"I don't care about biotech," I say. "All right? I don't care. Just because I'm good at it doesn't mean I have to force myself to do it for the rest of my life. And how good can I really be at it if I'm not invested in it?"

"You don't care," my mother says, as if she has to say it herself to understand. "And you suddenly care very deeply about botany."

"Yes. I do." This is a lie. In truth, I simply love Dr. Portsmouth's company. "At least, more than I care about what I've been doing for the past four years. What exactly is so important about all that? There are other people who can do it even better than I can."

"We're not talking about a field," my mother says, and I recognize her work face from the network broadcasts, the face she gets when a fellow lawmaker questions something fundamental to her position. "We're talking about the future. The people on this ship will never find a home on this planet we spent centuries traveling to unless we're willing to do one of two things. Either we terraform the atmosphere into oxygen, and thereby wipe out whatever millions of years of undiscovered evolution there is down there, or we tailor ourselves to be able to survive as a part of it. Life on Helena has come too far for the Law of Dignity to allow terraforming. That may not be clear to most people yet, but it will be before long. As soon as we see what's living in the oceans, there won't be any question. That leaves only one option. We have to evolve ourselves. There's no other way into the ecosystem without collapsing it altogether. There's no other way to have a home here."

My father listens with his elbows on the table, his palms flat together, fingertips leaning on his lips, and his eyes closed. Sometimes I watch his thinking with deep admiration and other times I wish he'd hurry up and say what he wants to say.

"I happen to have a home I like very much," I say. "Her name is the *Euclid*. And correct me if I'm wrong, but I thought it was decided way back at Midflight that colonization was not the be-all and end-all of this society."

My mother looks at me with a face I've never seen, a wide-eyed and angry yet frozen, placid calm like a fragile layer of ice on a lake, solid and serene but ready to crack at even a gentle touch. "Midflight," she says, "was a crime against dignity. What does a ship of trained conflict resolvers do when irreconcilable differences arise? They revert to their selfish, power-loving roots and stomp out dissent by refusing to compromise until no one feels free to disagree with them. If ever there was evidence that humans need to keep evolving, it's Midflight. Most people may be content to pretend it never happened, but I'm not."

I sit unable to move or speak, stupefied by this side of my mother that I never knew existed. She's always been a cave, hard to see into, worthy of caution, but suddenly I've learned a pack of wolves lives inside. My father brings down his hands and rests his forearms on the table. He opens his eyes and says, "Dolores."

My mother looks at him. She knows what he is thinking without him having to say a word.

He looks at her, and all I can picture is an exhausted black bear trying not to rile those wolves. He then looks at me. "If you want to understand where your mother is coming from," he says, "you should go with her on one of her Monday nights."

Grateful for a chance to move on from how strong a force of nature each of my parents is, I slip pieces together in my mind. Mondays, my mother attends meetings of the Children of Midflight, a group that all these years I had simply thought was a political lobby she visited so that she could represent a balanced point of view in her lawmaking—that's the story she's always told me. And minors, by law, have been barred from attending such groups until our objective knowledge base has developed enough to avoid non-consensual indoctrination. For the same reason, I've never been legally able to attend a religious service, though the strange notion of committed belief in something intrinsically unprovable has always fascinated me. Now that I'm eighteen, though, I can consent to being indoctrinated into whatever belief system I want, so long as its practice isn't an affront to the Constitution.

I look from my father to my mother and say, "Maybe that's a good idea."

My father picks up his fork and resumes eating. My mother and I can't follow quite so quickly, as if the air is still full of some dangerous dust best given time to settle, but after a minute of sitting and staring at our food, we get hungry.

#

The next few days flash by like particle accelerated in a collider, with data on every front streaming in from the labs to the network and into our classrooms, available to everyone from the most veteran researchers to the prodigies in Prime School. Analysts can barely keep up with the patterns their computers find because the new data keep modifying everything often and quickly. A problem assigned in a morning fourth-year Path School Bio class becomes outdated by evening. Students come to classrooms excited to see new discoveries, and teachers come ecstatic to share them. People in the corridors carry network screens, reading the news, whose writers struggle to sort through the heaps of incoming lab reports and organize them for easy perusal by the populace.

Five days pass. I accept the apprenticeship. I graduate from Path School, a ceremony whose grandeur pales when compared to achieving orbit, to discovering a wholly alien biology, and to getting the colony's next stage of history off to a running start. We new alumni throw our caps to the sky in the Deck One Park, and like all of our probes and satellites and spectrometers they fill the air, fly like a flock of the birds we've never seen, and fall back to us like the rain we've never felt. Everyone itches to set foot on the planet below, but can do so only in simulations. Two sets of triangulating satellites provide data for two simulators that run all hours of day and night for pure enjoyment, the rest in constant use for data collection. Colonists without access to lab simulators wait in line for hours to see what the planet feels like.

I don't. I know that starting tomorrow, when I begin my apprenticeship, I will get to see these things every day, all day, and all night if that's what observation requires. From my friends and cousins, I hear stories of the views from mountaintops and islands and rocky valleys, and I hear talk of the types of organisms spotted in the oceans so far, and debate about what levels of complexity are covered under the Law of Dignity. The desire to colonize, to free our population from containment in a spacecraft, appears and reappears on public broadcasts, but always the person speaking is older, someone who has spent half a lifetime or more waiting for this, never a newly legal adult like me, who was born during late deceleration.

And tonight, the evening before my first day in the simulator, I walk with my mother to a meeting of the Children of Midflight, no longer in my cap and gown but dressed in a casual, colorful blouse and loose, comfortable slacks. My mother, still in her formal pant suit from graduation and looking even more like a politician than usual, nevertheless walks with a more relaxed gait, shoulders loose and arms hanging freely.

"I have to warn you," she says, with an almost sly smile, the anger from a week ago disconcertingly absent, "it won't be like any network broadcasts you've seen. This is a community whose members stand in solidarity with each other, and who also know when not to take themselves too seriously. We know who we are, and where we came from, and we're hopeful about where we're going. Our meetings are more about preserving our history and identity than anything else. But that has a necessarily political element, with a clear political agenda. And tonight, you're in for a treat."

"Something special?"

"Tonight is a 'speak out' night. People tell personal or historical stories, share written work, even give performances if they feel like it. Tonight you'll get much more culture than activism, though many would question that distinction."

"How many people is it?"

"A lot of people have been busier since we reached orbit, so it'll be fewer than it has been. We used to have over a thousand members, with an attendance of at least three hundred a week, and every member attending at least once a month. Now it's likely to be maybe a hundred fifty."

We walk in silence for a moment, before I say, "I might not agree with some of this."

She stops and looks at me. "Our views result from history, both documented and inherited through oral tradition. You can disagree with whatever opinions you want, but the facts are the facts, and you won't be able to ignore them. What you're taught in school is in a sense objective, but by refraining from interpreting it, the teachers do it a disservice. Here, you'll find interpretation abounds, and you'll have to decide for yourself about its validity."

Not feeling at all prepared, I say, "I'm ready."

"You won't regret it," she says. She squeezes my hand.

We arrive at the doors to the meeting hall, and a warning flashes on them: Caution: Low-gravity environment. Vitals recorded.

"Okay, that I wasn't expecting," I say.

"We know how to have a good time," Mom says.

We go through the doors and find ourselves standing in a clear, spherical shell a little bigger than a maglev pod. The room beyond is a much larger sphere big enough to fit hundreds of people—it has a radius of at least fifty feet, I can't help calculating—and once the doors close behind us, the smaller sphere we're in rotates so that we can walk out onto the one continuous wall that is the room's floor and ceiling. This inside surface has been set on a nebula panorama, and as we step onto it, the pressure of our shoes makes a couple of projected asteroids spin over and hover rotating under us to make it look like we have something to walk on besides space. All around us people stand mingling with food and drinks, playing acrobatic low-gravity games, some strenuous to keep blood pressure from dropping in the low grav environment, and most people also listening to the speaker. In the center of the sphere, a man sits on a small platform atop a fifty-foot pole, visible to everyone who looks up, or down, depending on whose vantage point you take—inside a sphere, up and down are relative. From our position, the man perched in the sphere's center looks upside down as he rants:

"And what they don't say on that burning warning on the door is that your vitals are monitored everywhere, not just here. And sure, we know that—but it's rhetoric! It makes us feel like surveillance is necessary. Not to insult the doctors and the fine people on call who come running whenever somebody decides to stay in low grav without doing enough cardio. I mean, nobody wants to get hurt. What I do reject, most proudly, is the need to reassure us that surveillance is good. Surely if that were true, you'd think we wouldn't care whether we were being monitored. But surveillance breeds the consolidation of power. Before you know it, they'll be sending us warnings about our heart rate while we're enjoying a little rock of the boat.

Anybody ever hear of a computer saving someone's heart through coitus interruptus?"

The crowd laughs a little. My mother shakes her head, and her hair shakes behind it in slow motion from the lower gravity. "You'll hear some more cogent thoughts soon, I promise. This guy's clearly been celebrating, no offense to his dignity."

"Have you ever spoken?" I say. The low gravity makes walking a less convenient motion, so instead we gently skip, each step launching us forward ten feet or so toward a table of people. I assume she knows them, as I for some reason assume she knows every last person here.

"I do enough of that on the broadcasts," she says.

At the table I see one or two faces I recognize, friends who have been over to dinner in the past.

"This is my daughter, Edwyn Santiago," my mother says. "It's her first time here."

There's a wave of smiling and nods of recognition. Everyone stands, and several people offer congratulations on my graduation. Had everyone known who I was already? I smile and say thank you to all who shake my hand or kiss the air next to my cheek. It feels like a family reunion, but because it's mostly with people I've never met, my smiles aren't totally genuine. What is it that binds everyone here together?

"I've never heard much detail about all this," I say. "Who are the Children of Midflight?"

"You are," a woman my mother's age says. "And so am I, and so is everyone on this ship. Most of them simply don't know it. All of us are descended from the colonists who lived during the Midflight referendums. Everyone who voted 'no' on any of those decisions was victimized when the decisions were 'yes.' I know it sounds outrageous, but it's true."

She sips her drink, using a straw because of the low gravity. "Let me tell you what that man means by rhetoric. None of the Midflight ballots, not one, phrased its question in such a way that voting 'yes' would be in favor of the minority. You had to vote 'no'; you had to be acting in opposition. It couldn't be 'should the colony change its mission,' but 'should the colony continue as stated in the constitution.' It sounds little, but that's one example of many that you won't find pointed out in the historical record. You can read the questions yourself. What it adds up to, and forgive me if I go on, is that the minority view, while ostensibly given equal consideration, was actively discriminated against by majority lawmakers during the decision-making process, in an attempt to bring swing-voters over to their side. It was a fear tactic, it was unconstitutional, and the halfhearted attempts to address the concerns of the minority following the decision were laughable, no offense to the dignity of anyone involved, but plenty of offense to their actions."

She takes a breath, then shakes her head. "The people who raised me, and the people who raised them, all the way back to Midflight, are the people whose needs didn't count and who were ignored. It's been two hundred years and they still don't acknowledge this in the history books. Research with this view is deemed an 'alternative' interpretation, as if less valid than the norm. People want to believe the *Euclid* has been a perfect colony since its inception, but the truth is, what little perfection there may have been had eroded long before Midflight. Since then, it hasn't been the same."

My mother says to her, "You could have climbed up to that stool just now."

She waves a hand to dismiss the comment. "Please. I've been up there enough. I ought to propose a referendum on teaching a truly neutral history—I really should. But that one died a long time ago."

"It'll come," my mother says. She glances at me. "You never know when a new generation might listen. Especially now."

The woman smiles, and says to me, "We haven't been waiting just for this planet—and I swear, after this, I'll shut up—we've been waiting for history to recognize we exist. A whole segment of the population that wanted to go back to Earth, and was overruled: that, my dear, is who the Children of Midflight are."

On the low-grav game court nearby, women and men of wide-ranging age jump through high hoops by leapfrogging off each other's shoulders and somersaulting in slow motion through the air, twisting and diving like fish on the way down and landing in theatrical poses. It looks like a lot of fun, and not the least bit strenuous, requiring much less strength and skill than such a game in a normal-grav environment. Also much less skill than the group next to them who stands in a circle tossing a multitude of lightweight hand-sized spheres straight up and seeing how many they can keep in the air, everyone twisting this way and that, collectively juggling what must be hundreds of the balls. I used to play this game in Prime School to improve coordination and teamwork.

"Dad doesn't come here," I say to my mother. "Why is that?"

She stands next to me watching the games. "He did, years ago. He knows what there is to know. It's not really his scene."

A hush falls. I look up to see why. The ranting man has descended from the high seat, and a smaller, much older man pulls himself up, nearly flying by grabbing every tenth rung of the ladder; a quick push of the hand and he simply sails.

"This," my mother says, "is what I came for. You know who that is?"

The fluctuating nebula scene on the sphere's inside surface has taken a darker hue, and I can't make out the man's face. Only that he is bald and bearded.

"That's Raj Ramakrishnan," she says.

I recognize the name. Where have I heard it? My great-grandmother has mentioned it. He's one of the few people on the ship who's lived longer than she has. In fact, it comes to me now: he's the oldest colonist aboard.

"Is he here every week?"

"Every Speak Out, he's here."

The Helena Orbit

The hush deepens. The gnarled old Indian adjusts himself on the seat and then takes a slow look around, above and below himself.

"Here we are," he says. "In orbit."

A cheer rises from the crowd, and a wave of tension fills my body at the reverence they have for this one man's every word. It echoes historical images of Midflight itself, of the opposition leaders and the people who followed them without dissent. But I remember my objectivity, and listen.

"A hundred years ago I didn't much think we'd make it. I was young then. I thought, the closer we got, the more people would fight. It seems I was wrong. And that perhaps means there's a chance. Not a soul from my parents' generation thought colonization would ever be an option. But let me tell you a story. That's what I do best.

"The story begins in this very generation, the people now living, the people born during deceleration. We must decide, eventually, whether we can ever go down to this planet. The answer is, we can. And we will. And this is how it's going to happen.

"Our generation will be the first to redesign human biology. I know people still say it's too risky with the limited gene pool. But because we're here, at Helena, that no longer matters. It will start small. Some tweaks to metabolism, to respiration. If we're not going to kill everything down below, we've got to learn to breathe CO_2. And we will. Maybe we can find a way to separate the carbon out of it, turn it into glucose, like plants do, and get our oxygen from water. But transforming our bodies to live on Helena is only the beginning. It's the first real step we'll take in controlling our evolution. We've been content for hundreds of thousands of years to let mutations decide how we adapt, even though mutations are just as likely to kill us."

A barb of fear stings through me as I think of Haruko, ill from some contaminant triggering just such a dangerous mutation, probably from a gene humans didn't even have on Earth. The doctors still don't know how to cure her.

Ramakrishnan continues: "But we don't need to let mutations kill us anymore, and once we take that first step, many more will follow. The generation after ours, who are born able to survive in CO_2, will be free of the inhibiting fears we've been harboring, and will continue the work of adapting themselves to their environments under the guidance of our colony's accumulated knowledge. They will have freedom to evolve in ways we've only conceived of and written off as too difficult, even though researchers here on this very ship have made more progress in bioengineering than any of us ever expected. Every time we open the network, we're using a mix of electronic and biological technology, and we don't even think about it. But these new humans will.

"Eventually, maybe as soon as a generation after that, we'll be so practiced that whenever a change in the environment or ecology happens, a genetic adaptation for our children won't be far behind, no matter how radical the change may be. And, maybe as soon as a generation after that, we won't even have to wait for those who come after us to see these adaptations happen. We'll be able to alter the genetic code of grown adults. And that's where the real fun begins. You'll be able to wake up in the morning, go on the network, and see what new genes are available today. To pick whichever ones you want, to decide your own, personal evolution. Healing genetic diseases and regenerating damaged body parts will happen in a matter of seconds. You could have a hole blown in you by a meteorite and be able to put yourself back together.

"And while we refine the design of our own bodies, we'll be refining our bio-computers, too. We'll design them so that we can interface with them by touch and see their data in our minds. You know what happens the generation after that. We don't even need the computers anymore, because we've incorporated them into our own genes. We'll have wireless access to the network of our group consciousness, and can connect and disconnect at will.

"The generation after that, we'll move beyond bio-computer incorporation to other kinds of biotechnology in our bodies. We'll be able to engineer genes that are themselves capable of engineering genes, with the result that we can make changes to our own genetic code as we sleep or wake. We'll upload the programs for our new genes to the network and share them with anyone who's interested, or even physically pass our genes to one another with the shake of a hand or with a kiss. If hands or kisses still exist, that is. I'm sure some people will hold onto them for sentimental reasons.

"But the truth is, at that point we can turn ourselves into solar-powered beings that rarely, if ever, need to eat. We can make ourselves reproduce asexually, or simply not age. There may not be another generation after that, because there may not need to be. We can retain whatever parts of the male and female forms of humanity are useful, and do away with whatever we don't like. At that point, being human will mean something different than what it means now. It will simply mean having this ability to self-evolve, and whatever form you happen to take is irrelevant. What will matter will be that you can direct your own growth. And we will. We'll become a million different creatures with a million different forms, even capable of living in the vacuum of space, of extracting fuel from the stars themselves to travel at nearly the speed of light using whatever biological accelerator we've designed for ourselves that moment.

"And then, Children of Midflight, then will we have our autonomy. Then, of one mind, we can go, whoever of us choose to, back to Earth. We can see what will have become of the humans there, greet them as their distant relatives, though they will not recognize us. Even so, we will go home to that beautiful planet whose sun spawned our ancestors, and live, at last, as a free and dignified people."

He smiles. "Let that be all I say to you today. Grace and dignity to you always."

Everyone applauds, and after a moment so do I. Not knowing the nature of the strange feelings coursing my body, not able to consider to what extent I agree or don't agree with Ramakrishnan's vision, like everyone around me I applaud because I am affected. I turn to my mother, who stands holding herself, her eyes closed tightly, and my hands fall as if in normal gravity and then rise as I take her into my arms. I have no words to offer, but what she needs is clear. She holds me too, and I feel as if I am meeting her for the first time.

Five

I open my eyes to a sea of white and a torrent of wind, my clothes humming as they pull taut in the rush of air. I see only light, no point of reference for where I stand or sit or lie—my body floats freely, as if in space, but I laugh at the light and the wind. I am not anchored to any ground, and I do not fall. My body turns with the slowness of a planet, and nearby I sense some unfathomably large force. A horizon tilts into view, its surface miles below me, the features of the ground blurring with a speed that matches the wind. Mountains, valleys, forests, oceans rise over the vanishing point, whizz below, and blink out behind the opposite horizon.

Helena.

She spins faster than my eyes can follow. Frantic. Frantic as the wind. Her surface, what details I can briefly pick out from the dizzying panorama, is still. Inert. I am the mover. Still I laugh, no haste in my heart, because my speed sustains me. The air should wear my lateral velocity to nothing, but I do not slow. And maintaining speed, I maintain that endless fall I call orbit. Caught in gravity but only enough that I circle, a moth attracted to light but sane enough not to extinguish myself in yearning. The orbit cradles me, Helena's arms invisible, and in being held yet retaining the space to move, I can't keep from laughing on.

A moment of closed and then opened eyes reveals my dark bedroom walls, dark carpet, empty ceiling.

I fix the dream in my memory, replaying it until I'm sure I'll remember.

As soon as I sit up, the previous night returns. The *Euclid*'s half-hidden history, the Children of Midflight longing for home. My mother and I did not speak on the walk back afterward, but neither would we have refused to speak if one of us had found something to say. We watched the corridor ceiling turn from evening to night.

I find my mother at the breakfast table, with six different network screens stacked beside her plate of synthesized pancakes and mug of coffee.

"Good morning," I say, and she looks up, silent, searching for words.

"Good morning," she finally says, and smiles. She stretches one of the screens into a side table and stacks the rest of them there.

I consider describing my dream to her, but no summary does it justice. All I can think is, "There's something beautiful about orbit." But this sounds like a sentence she would smile at and dismiss, for she's more likely to find beauty in the matter-assembly of her breakfast than in a dream that defies the physics of atmospheric friction. She is not content to orbit Helena.

I'm sorry, a part of me wants to say. I'm sorry I disappointed you.

She puts down her fork and waits for me to say something, her face gentle, eyelids partly down.

I press my lips together. Another part of me believes I shouldn't apologize for my own agency. She watches me consider my words, and choose none of them.

I finally say, "Have you been to the simulators yet?"

"Not yet," she says.

That's all she wants to say, but I wait for her to go on.

She notices, and sips her coffee. "I don't know if I'm ready. What I really want is to set foot on real ground, not an image on a floor. I want to reach out and feel the walls be gone. No ship. No rooms. Just open space."

I listen and nod. "I get that. Sometimes I don't want to leave when I visit the parks."

"It's more than that. On Earth people used to say 'indoors' and 'outdoors.' But the *Euclid* has no outdoors."

My parents' bedroom walls are often covered by projected Earth landscapes. I've never taken the special comfort in them that she does.

"The simulator will only make it worse," she says. "I'm not interested in that. Not until we get closer to colonization."

I take a long breath, unaccustomed to her political candor. But it feels, at least, like a thick wall has come down.

"I'll read more about Midflight," I tell her. "I'll learn what there is to learn."

She smiles, the way she does whenever I tell an exciting story from school, but her pleasure quickly fades. She takes another sip from her mug. "You won't look at this colony the same way."

I shrug. "I guess we'll see."

I glance at the time on one of her net screens and jump up. "Time to go to work." I grab a nutrient bar from the assembler.

"Have fun," my mother says. "Work hard." She is trying to let me be me, but has yet to banish sorrow from her voice.

I swallow my first bite of breakfast, bend over, and hug her from behind. It's halfhearted, but I need her to feel that I'm not so far away. I say, "I'll see you later."

Without giving her time to respond, I hurry out into the corridor.

#

Pamela says, "Just sit tight. The satellites are almost in position."

I stand on a square treadmill that keeps me in one place no matter what direction I walk, and stays still when I do. The lab, smaller than I expected, contains little more than the components of the simulator I stand on and wear over my skin and, in a moment, over my eyes. Various screens and data-processing hardware line the walls, and Pamela sits in a chair at her workstation, controlling the satellites that fly as a team to deliver the

3D data. It's no wonder she can come to work in an old lab coat instead of a skinsuit when the work we do is completely digital. I wait for the data stream, flexing my fingers in the motion-tracking gloves, not used to having my hands contained so tightly. The data stream has yet to start, so when I pull down my eyewear I see nothing but its black insides. The virtual touchdown point today is the edge of a forest on the northern continent, the transitional land between two densities of vegetation signaling the border between different regions of the ecosystem.

"Here it comes," Pamela says.

The image fades in. The sky, a cloudless blue paler than Earth's because of the thicker atmosphere, stretches over me and down to a valley of red rock dotted with white shrubs. On the horizon, hazy mountains striped with varieties of rust and burnt umber slope up in a mixture of curves and corners. It resembles some of the desert landscapes of Earth, with only the hardiest plants surviving the harsh climate. Sounds are approximated, but on this windless day nothing moves. I stand and breathe and take in the view for a minute, imagining that I am no longer in orbit, but here, a visitor on the surface. What can I learn? What has Helena grown in her lengthy life?

Pamela sees a flat version of my feed on one of her screens, so we can have two pairs of eyes on everything. I turn on the network overlay, and labels of species whose identification has been posted online appear in small text hovering in the air.

"What do you think?" Pam says.

"It's pretty empty," I say. "Not literally, I mean . . . I see a lot of varieties of shrub, but they're few and far between." I crouch down for a closer look at the soil, which is sandy and full of pebbles. "The soil looks rough. Not sure I'd even call it soil."

I look in a slow circle at the ground to give Pam's more practiced eyes a look, until she says, "Stand up. Turn around."

I do, facing away from the valley now. A totally different sight greets me.

I stand at the bottom of a slope. Creeping down it from a pass between two nearby rock formations that stretch up into ridges of mountain, a forest of branching trunks and twisting roots stands as if frozen in the act of spilling into the valley. I walk toward it, around twenty paces up, until Pam says, "Stop. Look at the ground."

I crouch again. Finger-sized nubs of what looks like the same forest plants poke up from between the pebbles. Tiny trunks with branches and clusters of bulbs like the alveoli inside my lungs, colored a dull purple. Berries, spores, or what plants here have instead of leaves? I look at the valley again. The shrubs have flatter, much more leaf like clusters on their branches.

"What do you make of this?" I say.

"The seedlings, if that's what they are, look healthy, or at least look like the adult specimens," Pam says. "Presuming the larger ones are in fact the adults. Too soon for any guesses as to why it hasn't spread further. Take a closer look at one of the larger trunks."

I climb further up the slope, a little disoriented by the still flat surface under my feet, and the nubs climb to shin height, then knee height. The species has been identified by a number on the network, but hasn't yet been classified in any biological kingdom for certain. The knee-high specimens look nearly the same as the seedlings, with bulb clusters the same size, and branches spaced the same way that split in the same patterns. But here, roots run in and out of the ground in snakelike tendrils, and many of the smaller specimens sprout from these roots.

"See how all the roots run in the same direction?" Pam says. "They could extend under the ground for quite a ways. In fact, I'd bet the smallest specimens are all growing from the same root system."

"Then you mean they aren't seedlings," I say. "Just the edges of something like a ground-covering vine?"

"That's a possibility, though I never met a vine that grew trunks like these. Let the biologists worry about classification. More important, look at the soil here."

I do, and wonder if she sees something I don't. "It looks the same to me."

"Me too. I'll have to request some data on what it looks like deeper down, to see if there's something we're missing. But don't expect results on that anytime soon. The Bio and Astrophysics departments have been slow in determining what types of radiation are safe to use on this ecosystem. They want to collect data on the natural background levels for a few more days at least. So we have to make the most of our eyes until then. From what I've seen so far, it could also be that when it rains, this species prefers higher altitude and dryer ground. Or it could be a combination of a hundred such factors."

"Better observe some more, then."

"Exactly. Take a look at the larger trunks, the ones as tall as you."

As I get closer to the forested zenith of the slope, a quick quiver of nervousness unexpectedly pinches my chest. It is so quiet. The treelike specimens stand strong and tall, but I feel more as if I am approaching a sleeping animal than a forest, maybe because I know so little about what I see. I keep waiting for a gust of wind like in the Earth simulations, but nothing comes. Somehow this feels more like pre-colony Mars, yet not so long dead as that planet had been. I walk among truly alien life forms, invisible to them but for the twinkle of our ship and our satellites in the sky after nightfall.

"The roots are bigger," I say, absently, certain Pam has already noticed. "Everything else looks the same, exactly the same. It's definitely just one species as far as I can tell."

"Even that's too much to say for sure," Pam says. "Don't worry about conclusions. Just keep observing data. We have all the time in the world for this."

I reach out and touch one of the tree trunks, the skinsuit pushing back, approximating the pressure I apply.

"That's it," Pam says. "Just get to know this place. Get familiar with it. Notice details, no matter how insignificant, so you can tell when something changes."

"Some of the trunks connect," I say. Up ahead the data is lower-resolution and pixelated, because the satellites can't see beneath the branches from their current positions.

"Let me adjust the satellite focus," Pam says. "We should be able to approximate the forest floor pretty accurately in a second."

The pixels shrink until the image clears. I duck between two trunks that stand taller than I do, and step into the forest. "Wow," I say.

The trunks cluster in clear, even patterns, in what look like multiples of three, growing from a floor that is all root and no soil, the sunlight dappling through. In the smaller groves, the berrylike clusters are darker, like the smaller specimens, but take on a paler hue in the groves with twelve trunks or more. The ground slopes in rolling hills and waves of roots that look much thicker than the trunks they sprout.

"This is incredible," I say.

"Look at everything," Pam says. "All our data will go on the network. Take your time."

I step over roots and approach one of the groves. The trunks grow slanted out as if they all extend from a single node below the surface, unlike the trunks at the edge, which grow straight up.

"I wonder why the distribution is so uneven in the smaller ones," I say. "This is so much more patterned."

"Time may tell," Pam says.

"I can't even see a hint of what the ground is like here. It's completely dominating the landscape."

"Sound familiar?"

"I don't know what you mean."

"Think of Earth. Think of cities."

"That's true. But you don't think these were cultivated this way?"

"I don't think anything," Pam says. "Get out of conclusion mode. This isn't a lab experiment. This is pure observation. I'm just making connections, noticing ways in which the system looks similar to other systems I've seen."

"I wonder why the clusters of bulbs are paler in the large groves."

"A good question, but what do you need to do with it?"

I think. "Let it remain a question. Until I observe more."

"That's my girl. Want to do a little rock climbing?"

"Where?"

"Back where you came in. Climb up one of those formations."

I follow my steps back toward the valley, and pass between the same two trunks on my way out.

"Now just walk up one side. Step forward, and you'll slide right up it."

The red rock face looms steep enough to lean on, and walking up it without difficulty, I acutely feel the unreality of the simulation and also feel the vast distance that exists between me and the place I explore. I can stand on a nearly vertical slope and not slide down.

On reaching higher ground, I look out to the next valley, which the forest covers.

Nothing but purple, the plants carpeting this valley from edge to edge. Even the lower, more rounded mountains on the far end of this valley wear a violet blanket. Beyond them, more distant mountains on the hazy horizon take a purple tint.

I ask, "Is it fair to say we've found a candidate for the dominant species of this ecosystem?"

Pam says, "You tell me."

"Not until we observe more?"

She laughs. "Now you've got it."

#

After work, I head to one of the parks to meet Hesper and Isaac, almost skipping down the corridor. Hesper's lab, with its own set of satellites, has been imaging the oceans today in search of the largest sea creatures, and also organisms at the microbiological level, using the one imaging satellite capable of that level of magnification. It may not be long before her lab unveils the lynch pin that holds Helena's biosphere together: the mechanism by which complex life somehow evolved without oxygen. Isaac's lab in astrophysics samples the radiation levels and studies Helena's orbit, gravity, and planet-sun environment. They're the ones the rest of us are waiting on to see if it's safe to go beyond mere imagery and into deep scanning.

I swim down two decks through a zerograv chute and slip out into a concourse where people sit and eat, looking through large windows into the park, whose projected sky shows a sun in late afternoon, nearly evening. Still in my white lab skinsuit, I key in the number for a sleeveless sun dress. I cross the threshold into the park, a grassy plot with small ups and downs in the ground, lots of trees, and a pond in the middle. No sidewalks here, which always makes me feel giddy and I remove my shoes. I walk barefoot on the green and set my shoes back into their marble and pocket it.

The fake sun warms my shoulders. I wander through the trees until I spot my friends standing near the pond. I walk down the grassy bank to meet them.

"Hey you," I say to them.

They turn, the pond sparkling behind them and throwing curves of light up and down their bodies. They still wear lab clothing, their faces tense. I stop walking.

"What's wrong?"

Isaac opens his mouth, but says nothing.

"We tried to call you," Hesper says.

I had turned off messages while at work and had forgotten to re-enable them before I left the lab. "Sorry," I say. "What happened?"

Isaac turns back to the water, holding himself.

"Haruko's in the hospital again," Hesper says. "It's not looking good."

"How bad?"

Hesper shakes her head. "Don't know."

I run a hand over my face. "I thought they were close to isolating the causes."

"They are. But it might be . . ." She looks at the grass. "It might not be enough."

"Have you seen her?" I ask.

Isaac crouches on the pebbles by the water, hands still clutched to his elbows.

I squat beside him, put a hand on his back, and move it in slow circles. He shows no response to my touch, looks only at the water.

"There's no space for anyone in the room with her," Hesper says. "You can see in though."

The brown skin of Isaac's face shines in the sun, his eyes red. I move my hand from his back to around his far arm and squeeze him close. He closes his eyes and shakes. I hold him hard.

A gust of wind blows through, warm and comfortable. Hesper raises her head into it, and her hair flies every direction. The afternoon light casts stark shadows everywhere, a stunning contrast that brings out shapes and depth.

I stroke Isaac's back once more, and stand up.

"I have to go see her," I say.

Hesper nods. "Call me if you need to talk." Her face shows no emotion but solemnity, but her arms, limp at her sides, give away something deeper.

"I will," I say.

I take the marble from my pocket and put on my shoes, the grass feeling suddenly annoying on the soles of my feet. In the concourse, I hop into a maglev and ride it to the hospital deck, waking from a daze when it finally stops.

I talk to the hospital receptionist briefly, and he gives me directions, warning me I won't be able to see much, and that she's been getting a lot of visitors, so I may have to wait. I walk through empty, narrow corridors, turn corners, follow signs on the walls, and end up in a waiting room full of grim colonists of all ages. I spot Haruko's parents and go to them instead of to the room's receptionist. They stand and hug me. I can tell they have been crying, their faces sagging with exhaustion.

"Can I see her?" I say.

"I'll take you," her mother says.

She leads me out of the waiting room and down a hall, stopping before we reach a window. I look through. Haruko lies in bed, her body covered with monitors and readouts. She breathes through a tube. Her face has taken the sickly green tint much more darkly than before.

I look back at her mother, but she's leaving, already halfway down the hall.

Two doctors walk about in the room with Haruko, speaking words I can't hear, checking screens and workstations, and adjusting various settings on her skinsuit. I imagine her having nightmares while trapped under all that equipment, but it's likely she's sedated enough that she won't dream.

She managed to finish her symphony while dealing with this, unyielding. I refused to go into bioengineering because I merely don't enjoy it.

"She'll make it," a voice startles me. Rio. Has khe been there the whole time?

"I hope so," I say. "She doesn't look good."

"She's strong."

I know this, know this as well as anyone, and it feels oddly insulting to hear it from someone else.

"You two know each other well," I say.

"We did," khe says, looking through the glass at Haruko.

"You love her?" In the face of losing her, tact seems not to matter.

"Don't you?"

"I mean . . . as more than a friend."

"I could not call her family."

Yes, then, or no? Why does khe have to be so cryptic? "She never told me about your piece of the counterpoint. She told me everything, I thought."

"She's an enigma."

"So are you." I say it more indignantly than I intend.

Khe blinks at me. "In what way?"

I look away. "I don't know. I can't figure you out."

I feel Rio watching me.

"Maybe it's just me," I say. And I think: I'm looking for something that isn't there.

"Do you want to take a walk?" khe says.

A hundred versions of "why" and I discard them.

"There's a zerograv sphere I like," khe says. "It helps me relax."

"I might get sick," I say. "I already feel sick."

Rio nods. Khe leaves the window behind and shrinks down the hallway.

"I could use a walk though," I say. Khe stops. I catch up, and massage my shoulder as we walk. "I'm really tense."

"You look it."

"I must be a mess."

Khe shrugs. "You look neat enough. Even if you didn't, appearance matters little to most people."

"That's what everyone says. Except my mother. She takes pride in the way she looks."

I stop on the way out to hug Haruko's parents again and thank them for showing me in. Then Rio and I leave the waiting room, taking the shortest route we can find out of the hospital.

"It's interesting, culturally," khe says. "No one in my family values appearance beyond practicality. Or at least, no one makes a point of doing so."

"Sounds boring."

"I don't think I've ever been bored."

"Well you know what I mean. Looking the same every day."

"Do I?"

"I guess so. You're always wearing your lab clothes."

"It helps me keep my objectivity in mind."

"I can identify with that." I joke, "But objectivity doesn't exist, you know," referencing Prime School philosophy lessons.

"But striving for it is important," khe says, playing along. Then, more seriously, "I do strive for it. Diligently."

"That's only your opinion," I tease.

"Opinions are nothing but premature conclusions. All of the destructive acts in history arose from opinions that people considered to be fact."

Okay, touchy subject. "But what about fun? Don't you ever laugh?"

"Of course."

"And it's subjective! There's no such thing as an objectively hilarious joke."

"It's an emotional response, not a position arrived at through logic."

"What about beauty? Don't you find anything pretty?"

"That's also an emotional response, of appreciation. Nothing is objectively pretty."

"You sound like a computer."

By now we've exited the hospital and I follow Rio wherever khe may be going. Khe stops, then keeps walking. "If nebulae could speak, what would a particularly appearance-obsessed nebula say if it was about to collapse under its own gravity and form into stars, presuming the nebula would prefer to remain a nebula?"

I frown for a second. "I don't know."

"'I need to lose some weight.'"

I smile despite the abysmal quality of the joke. "That's really bad."

"In what way?"

"I don't know." I'm laughing now. "It's just . . . terrible. It's completely forced."

"Your logic is at odds with your emotional response. It makes you laugh, but you consider it unfunny. Because you're aware your laugh response is subjective."

"I don't see the point you're trying to make."

"Emotional responses are still objective in the sense that they can be observed. I suppose my point is that more objectivity is possible than you think. If a second observer had said that you didn't in fact laugh, that would cast doubt on the objectivity of . . ."

"Okay, I get it. And the point *I'm* trying to make is . . . I don't know. I guess you'd come across to me as less of an enigma if you showed a little more emotion. But that's selfish. I guess that's not who you are."

We walk down the corridor.

"Have you ever been to a religious service, or a political rally?" I ask.

"I've observed some. Never participated."

"I went to a really interesting one last night, with my mother. Do you know of the Children of Midflight?"

"I've heard the name." Khe stops me in front of a door. "This is the zerograv room I was telling you about. How are you feeling?"

"Better. A little."

"Care to join me?"

"Only if we can keep the discussion . . . light."

Khe smiles. "A pun?"

"Made you smile."

Khe smiles wider. "I don't know if that's true. I didn't observe myself."

I push khen. "You!"

Khe laughs. A high, beautiful tenor, clear and smooth.

Khe opens the door and steps in. I follow. We stand on a small platform in a spherical room much like the one from last night, but smaller, only the size of an ordinary living room. A control screen shows the gravity and simulated location settings.

"Pick any location you like," khe says. I scroll through, but don't like any of them. I return to the main menu and set it on the ship's visual readout, and Helena appears, below us, her sun about to set behind her.

"Nice," khe says.

"I like it," I say. "It makes me feel like I'm part of the ship."

I set the gravity on zero. Set the room on private. The gravity drops, and already, from the motion of breathing, I begin to float. I remember my dress and change it to a pair of shorts for privacy, already feeling vulnerable by sharing this moment with Rio, by letting khen share it with me.

Below us, the platform retracts. I take off my shoes and pocket their marble. "You have a nice voice," I tell Rio. "Do you ever sing?"

"Not often." Khe floats nearby, but not too close.

"I sing in Choir every month," I say. "It's very . . . emotional, for me. I can't describe it."

The best part of zerograv is when I can manage to stop floating in any particular direction and simply hang there. I'm still drifting, the wall getting closer, the air not enough to slow me down. It's like floating on the surface of the water in a pool, if that surface was in three dimensions.

"Can you do me a favor?" I say. I have no idea where khe is now, somewhere behind me. I turn my head, and see khen floating curled, holding khes legs.

"What's that?" Rio says.

"Can you just . . . stop me? I don't need a big push; I just want to stop drifting."

"The walls are cushioned," khe says. "I think if you bounce once, you'll lose enough energy that you won't float very far."

"You think so?"

"I do this a lot. I know exactly what you're after. The stillness. If you wait for it, it'll come on its own."

"That's always the hardest part," I say. "I'm not very patient." Pam said patience was a necessity for working in her lab. I'll have to make myself patient, then.

I look up and see Rio bounce off the stars, gently, without moving any of khes limbs.

The wall comes at me, and I tense, releasing a little of the tension as the cushion takes me in, then slowly, delicately, it pushes me back out. The wall recedes, slows, and stops. I am still but for a slow spin. I savor it for a moment, curled up like Rio, but letting my muscles relax.

"I usually end up holding onto the wall, and then letting go," I say, softly so as not to give myself any more of a spin with my breath. "It's nicer in the center."

"Don't talk," khe says. "Let your spin wear out."

It takes a minute. My hair floats around me, getting in my eyes sometimes, and I close them. I feel my body growing slower, my exhalations going between my knees and chest. The lack of motion fills me up, a feeling surprisingly similar to the moments when one quarter of a four-part harmony is projecting from inside me and deepening the sounds of others. An ineffable comfort. I let my arms and legs uncurl ever so slowly, and I hang there, weightless and perfectly still.

I open my eyes. Helena's sun has set, and against the blue and orange crescent of her atmosphere, Rio's silhouette floats like an infant cradled in the womb of space.

Six

After the few minutes of inertness our bodies are allowed before our blood pressure drops in the low gravity and the network warns us about our need to move strenuously again, Rio and I part ways, wishing each other good night.

On the maglev ride home, the red tunnel lights remind me of the hallway outside Haruko's room, her readouts blinking. The doctors have already put out a bulletin on the network with images of her splitting skin, to see if any researchers come forward with a possible contaminant, anything to lead them to what caused inert genes to suddenly express themselves. They've already sequenced her genome several times trying to find clues.

The momentary rush of wind as the airtight maglev door opens makes me jump, and I climb out, walk the starlit corridor home, and call it a night.

#

I spend two hours tossing, turning, and trying everything from ambient noise and humidity and temperature adjustments to changing various bed densities. I get up and go to the living room. My father sits on a cushion, eyes closed, hands on his knees, probably in meditation. The room is a void, furniture subsumed into the blank, gray walls. The room completely on default settings.

I stand still, considering whether to let him be. He opens his eyes and turns his head toward me. He smiles, and speaks softly. "I didn't want to wake your mother."

Because my father counsels people, I know what to expect when I tell him certain things. Right now, I can use a little predictability. "I can't sleep. I'm worried about Haruko."

He uncrosses his legs with deliberate slowness as if they are precious, easily broken. Then he stands. I go to him and he holds me. Says nothing.

When I let go, he smooths my bed hair, then goes to the wall and uncovers the food dispenser. He flips through public listings until he finds an herbal tea blend by someone he knows. Chamomile and lavender, with a hint of sage. He bookmarks it, and brings two steaming mugs over to the table and chairs I'm forming from the floor. We sit.

"I did a kind of meditation earlier, I think," I tell him. "Zerograv. Have you ever managed to float while being totally still? It's the most relaxing thing."

"Not for me," he says. "Too short-lived. These nights I sit for a couple hours."

"Wow." I cup my hands around the warm mug. Breathe in the floral steam. "I've tried floating in the swimming pools, too, but not for hours at a time."

"You're still young," he says. "Once you finish apprenticing and get a few years of research in . . . life evens out. Nothing seems quite so urgent."

"I don't know if that's applicable to my generation," I say. I take a sip. This is better tea than any of the defaults. I can almost taste the colors of the plants that were brewed in it before it was scanned into the assembler. Purple, yellow, green.

He smiles. "So says every person on reaching your age. From your vantage point, the past four centuries must seem like the most boring tedium."

"I used to think so," I say. "I'm kind of afraid to read about Midflight."

"Tell me what you want to know."

I think briefly. "What's everyone so angry about? I mean, I understand that people wanted to go back to Earth and couldn't, but this 'crime against dignity' stuff Mom talks about feels a little strained. The referendums may have been phrased in a slightly biased way, but they were still offering a choice. People still voted."

"The voting itself was the problem," he says. "At least, that's what the most respected critics have said. Because the discontented were a definite minority, treating the problem as a numbers issue ensured they wouldn't get what they wanted. A few people, those most involved in policy, acted quickly to make sure the question of returning the ship to Earth would be voted on rather than resolved some other way. Many say their motivations weren't entirely pure. That they were shaping public opinion by even framing it as a referendum question."

I stare into my father's blue irises, crease-rimmed eyelids, the many intricate suggestions of age in his fifty-year-old skin, in his thinning hair. People here, *Euclid* people, of our own colony, used a referendum, the supposed epitome of democracy, to oppress?

My father, reading my face, says, "It was a different colony then. A different ship."

I say, "But how else could an issue like this be settled?"

"The argument then, as now, is that voting didn't settle a thing. All it did was legitimize the majority viewpoint and stigmatize the others. This argument was made, publicly, by the minority. Their broadcast was dismissed by prominent figures as the whining of those facing certain defeat. Not in so many words, but again, those who were accustomed to the spotlight took advantage of their privilege. While many who didn't want to return to Earth spoke up in favor of pursuing solutions other than referendum, many others found it easier not to get involved. But those well-versed in the Constitution knew that certain articles applied, and made excellent arguments against the referendums. I can give you names if you like."

My tea sits cooling as I gesture with my hands. "But then why did the referendums happen? Why didn't they have a referendum on whether to have a referendum? It's been done before."

"This is where only a visit to the network can help you. You're asking the right questions, but the only answer history offers is what happened, not why. I've been giving you a mix of fact and opinion, but from here on, I have little but opinion."

"Well, give me your opinion, then."

He holds his mug to his lips, inhales, but doesn't drink. He sets it back on the table. "Before Delerue discovered Helena's true atmospheric composition, people were mostly content. At least, we can't find much evidence that they weren't. That's fact. It's also documented that very few people, a minority, participated in the political process in the years leading up to Midflight. This speaks volumes to me. Messages back to the solar system had a forty-year lag and mostly stopped, and people were more interested in their research, their art, in anything but reminding themselves they would never see Helena. And up until Midflight, they'd gotten good at it. They didn't much notice or care that a few very ambitious people had become a de facto government by stepping up to do the lawmaking work no one else wanted to do.

"These people had no prestige, they had no material gain, but because of the apathetic populace, they did to an extent have power. And when people get power, they hold onto it. The Io colonists engineered the Constitution to prevent power's consolidation, but no matter how good your constitution may be, if people are largely content, as they were then, some people will be apathetic about politics, and some will be ambitious about finding ways to acquire what little power there is to get. Because of the sheer drama that unfolded during Midflight, the level of political participation increased drastically, and the democratic process straightened itself out. The people divided the power, and the faction that engineered the Midflight referendums became merely one voice among many others. As it should have been from the beginning."

I rock my mug back and forth, and watch the dregs get stirred up and settle. "Why didn't they teach us about this in Prime School?"

"Because, as I said, it's opinion. There have been great historians who have done meticulous gathering of sources, but nothing that says definitively that power was abused."

For reasons I can't explain, I am nearly in tears. "But there's been enough to convince you."

"Yes. But I bring my own biases to it. I have detailed opinions about the human psyche that color my interpretation of the facts, and that cause me to make connections which may not have, in reality, existed. Where facts are in doubt, you have to rely on experience. And now that you're done with school, there's a whole world of contested history, philosophical speculation, and even religion, which you won't be able to avoid completely. Sooner or later, you're going to have to form opinions about some big questions."

Rio's face, khes argument for objectivity, comes back to me. Was khes dedication to such objectivity a response to this? To encountering the *Euclid* outside the facts?

"The scientific method is a beautiful thing," my father says. "I used it as far as it would get me in psychology. But sooner or later you run into what I call the Wall of Doubt. The point beyond which there are no hard and fast answers. Morality? It's a matter of opinion. We have the Law of Dignity to guide us, and a good job it's done of correcting us when we go astray. But science can't tell you what's good or evil, or what belief system is best. I've explored every religion that's practiced on this ship, and experience is all I have to guide me in deciding what they're worth.

"What beliefs align my behavior with what I consider ideal? For that matter, what assumptions underlie what I consider to be ideal behavior?" He takes a sip of his tea. "You can go through life ignoring these questions, and you wouldn't be amoral to do so. Focusing mostly on scientific questions has made extraordinary things happen in this colony. But there's a reason we have an Artist Laureate, and it isn't because the writers of the Constitution proved scientifically that happy human societies need art. That will always be a matter of opinion. But it's one which I think we can agree, from experience, has made our lives richer."

The image of Haruko on the bed, smothered by apparatus, nearly brings tears back to my eyes. I fight them. "So now that I'm done with school I'm free to get indoctrinated into any irrational, baseless belief system I want? I can throw science and reason out into space? I feel like it's all I have."

"It's your only way of making sense of the universe," he says. "That's true. But other things can become additional ways. Some of the people you sing with in Choir are there because the act, the ritual of raising your voice in music, makes the universe more understandable to them than anything they learned in school does. The tea we're drinking comes from a woman I know whose happiness relies on creativity, on connecting with herself and others through what our bodies consume. At the end of the day, we're all still incomplete, emotional people. That's why Midflight happened, but it's also why Haruko's symphony happened. It's why we left Io in the first place, and it's why I do what I do."

I take a drink. The tea is barely warm now, but I taste it more vividly. I stand up, come around to my father, and in his arms take refuge from a world I no longer know.

#

In the morning I sit in my sphere to practice singing and keep my voice in shape for Choir. I flip through various compositions and find nothing that speaks to me. I eat breakfast next to my mother, but say only one or two words to her. I show up in Pamela's lab wearing baggy eyes and probably a scowl.

In her chair Pam swivels away from her console to face me. "You ready for some sunshine?" she says.

"I guess so."

"No grumbling," she says. "If you're gonna bring your bad mood into my lab, you can turn around. I'll go back to Io before I deal with another apprentice who won't work like a professional."

I snap myself out of it. "I'm sorry," I say. "I didn't sleep—"

"No excuses. Are you ready to work?"

"Yes, ma'am."

She smiles, and those disarming crow's feet come back around her eyes. "Keep your head on straight. I need you as a scientist, not a teenager, no offense to your dignity."

I set my clothing to the simulator skinsuit. "Why does being eighteen make you an adult, anyway?"

"If we set it higher, people would let themselves stay children that much longer. Again, no offense. I fall into the crank pit too sometimes, but I leave it in the corridor."

I take up the sim-goggles from their locker in the wall. "How many apprentices have you had?"

She turns back to her console and instructs the satellites. "Haven't been counting. Last one was a strong-headed case, and barely stable emotionally. Not sure what he had going on at home, but I'm sure it wasn't good. He ended up placed with different parents."

"I didn't think that happened anymore."

"You don't hear much about it unless you know someone involved. There's a lot that happens in the private places on this ship that stays secret."

"Like Midflight?" I step onto the simulator platform.

She stops typing, but stays facing her console. "Sounds like you've been looking into the abyss a little harder than most your age. Are you ready for the sim?"

"I am."

"All right, get to it. Data's coming now."

I pull down the goggles. "What's on the agenda?"

"I've been looking at that massive plant system and mapping what look like central nodes. We're about to take a closer look."

"How early did you come to the lab today?"

"Three."

"Burning Io."

"Aren't you glad you're just an apprentice?"

The landscape fills my vision. Everywhere the ground twists with gray root, a woody layer carpeting the forest of purple-nubbed branching trunks. But instead of rolling in smooth, small hills as before, the roots here slope up.

"Looks like it covered a mountain," I say.

"You might think so. But the topography is pretty clear from orbit. This particular rise in the ground is all organic."

"A mountain of just root?"

"Root and whatever else the subterranean part of the organism has. What looks like root to us could just be protection against the elements for something more delicate. There's no way to know yet. All the penetrating scans are still off limits until we get more data on background radiation."

I shake my head at that, then remind myself: patience. "Where do you want me to go?"

"Nowhere, yet. What else do you notice here?"

All around me the trunks rise more densely in clusters of nine, twelve, fifteen. They reach far higher, what was a roof before, now a distant canopy. I describe it to Pam.

"Good. Noticing anything else that's changed?"

I look around for a moment, comparing what's before me now to my memory of the previous sim. Most of the bulb clusters lie farther up the trunks, harder to get a good look at, but a few still poke out of the root-ground. Something is off. I look back up, count trunks here and there. I say, "In the last location, the large trunk clusters had paler bulbs on their branches. Here the smaller clusters are paler. What few of them I see, anyway."

"Exactly. I went into the simulator myself this morning, to yesterday's location. The sun was barely up, but I could tell immediately that there was no dark or pale. Everything was the same color. So I went over more data from yesterday, from one of the stationary orbital cameras. And I found a pattern."

"In the color?"

"It alternates. The large clusters turned pale in the morning and darkened in late afternoon, when the small clusters turned pale. At night, the large clusters paled again, and at dawn this morning they were switching places, the large darkening and the small lightening on a roughly six-hour schedule, leaving us with what you see now."

"And it was all synchronized? How far out?"

"No boundary. I spent hours looking for a break in the pattern—for any section following a different schedule. All small clusters on this continent turn pale at the same time, or darken at the same time. Same with the large ones."

I look downhill at the sea of purple forest below, and uphill at the larger and larger trunks. "I want to see what's at the top of this," I say.

"Go ahead."

I climb up, my feet sliding easily as I walk in place on the simulator platform. A strange sadness comes over me, and I wish I could actually climb this landscape, feel the true texture of these roots on my fingertips, breathe the real smell of this toxic air. Helena fills my vision, never closer and never more distant.

At the summit of this living hill stands a cluster of three trunks, each as wide as one of the *Euclid*'s corridors and reaching ten or fifteen stories high. I slip between two of the three trunks into the hollow where they all join together, again wishing I could exert myself in the process, pulling my body up with my own straining arms instead of striding calmly on a treadmill. I look up at the three towers above, their branching symmetry, nearly crystalline geometry. And looking down from the summit I see nothing but the tops of purple clusters vanishing into the hazy horizon no matter where I turn.

"What do you make of all this?" I say.

"Nothing," she says. "The most thrilling nothing I can imagine. We see here something truly unknown. A life form we may not understand in our own lifespan. Assuming a hundred different things we haven't proven, I would guess we're looking at a growth that's hundreds, if not thousands, of years old. What I've seen so far looks like the unchecked spread of an as yet unstoppable organism. Is it a single organism covering this whole continent? I don't know. It may be that what we see as the boundary between one organism and another may not even apply here. The only constant rule of biology is that survival requires energy. Everything else is up in the air. Even the definition of survival could be different. Maybe smaller organisms have been subsumed into this one. I could posit a hundred different theories, and only time, a lot of time, could disprove them."

"How will we ever figure this out without coming down here? For real? I want to . . . I want to touch this thing. I want to take samples. I want to see what's inside it."

"Radiological scans are our best bet for now. As soon as we're certain about the background radiation, we should be able to work within those parameters to get a look inside these things. But for all we know, even a little increase in X-rays might make it sick. That data should be coming soon. Trust me, I've been keeping an eye out."

"I haven't even had time to look at what people are discovering," I say.

"You have to keep yourself in the loop," Pam says. "That's a big part of this."

"I know."

"Guess how many views the video we took yesterday got when I put it on the network."

"Since yesterday? No idea."

"Tens of thousands. People are reading lab reports by the hundreds, and some actual video makes it much easier to see what everyone else is talking about. We're doing important work."

The Helena Orbit

I shift my weight, not sure how comfortable I feel with thousands of people looking out through my eyes, watching my feet and my hands.

"Tell you what," Pam says. "Why don't you hop out of the simulator and do some reading now. I'll keep working with the feed here at my console, and I'll ask you to jump in when I need a closer look at something."

"All right." I take off the goggles and step off the platform. The walls and ceiling of the lab feel tight and cold. My history teacher used to say that most people on Earth, or on one of the colonies, would recoil at the thought of living their whole lives in a closed box like the *Euclid*, that open space, if you're born with it, becomes crucial to the human psyche. If it weren't for the parks and low-gravity environments that allow us some room to move, then who knows, we might become like goldfish and eventually find our growth stunted by our walls, shrinking with each generation to give ourselves breathing space. Conjecture, sure, she used to say, but it shows the complexity of the way humans interact with our environments. Because we were all born with these walls and ceilings, and maybe even find comfort, security in them, none of us can know how it feels, for real, to stand on top of a mountain with nothing but air for miles. It might feel terrifyingly vulnerable.

I remember the vulnerability of the previous night again. The floating, silent but together. It strikes me how long it's been since I last went for a real swim in one of the ship's pools. Maybe after work today I can go. See if Hesper or Isaac—or Rio—wants to join me.

I look up the geology labs' findings since orbit, and look for Rio's name on the lab reports. They've completed their map of Helena's subterranean hotspots, still working on a map of all its active volcanoes, most of which lie under the cloud cover that stretches over the island region. Breaks in the cloud cover and infrared spectroscopy have, however, allowed mapping of many islands, some of which appear to be newly formed by active undersea volcanoes. The report notes that as soon as the planet's radiation levels have been tracked long enough to provide average daily highs and lows, work should progress much more quickly with the aid of radiological scans.

Same here, I think to myself. Looks like we're all waiting for that, not quite used to the limits of using our eyes alone. Isaac's got his work cut out for him.

I look at another lab report. The constant cloud cover suggests so many active volcanoes throughout the island region that before one cloud has cleared, another eruption occurs. That sounds eerily familiar. Is this a region of Helena not too unlike Io? That's sure to make a lot of colonists uncomfortable. Or to keep them uninterested in this region.

Rio, striving for objectivity, proceeds without such commentary in khes lab report, comparing the geological features discovered here more to those on Earth than to those on any colony. As if it doesn't even occur to khen to compare it to Io. Khe must be thinking about it, though. Who couldn't? Who on this ship doesn't feel the ghost of Io imprinted on khes unconscious?

I open a message tab and type Rio a few words: *Want to go swimming after work?*

I go to the marine biology team's reports while I wait for an answer. Their infrared scans of Helena's oceans have revealed a complicated mix of stationary lifeforms similar to planktons and moving clouds of pea-sized swimming creatures. Nothing large by Earth standards: no sharks, dolphins, whales, or anything larger than a fingernail. Given that all of these things evolved without significant oxygen in the atmosphere, though, with the acidity level of the ocean to boot, their complexity is unprecedented. Theories abound, but, the reports say, who would have guessed it, radiological scans are expected to provide quicker progress. Now I'm quite glad I'm not one of the people working in astrophysics this past month. Is every lab on the ship waiting to hear from them, banking that they'll be able to use backscatter X-ray or millimeter-wave scanners to see inside specimens? What a setback it will be if we can't safely use them at all.

The Helena Orbit

While scrolling through the various posts on the network, I come across a request for a crowdhack, calling for any available scientists—biologists, geneticists, and microbiologists especially—to lend a hand at solving a problem. It's from the hospital deck, and next to the description of the patient's symptoms are several images of Haruko's skin condition. They're running out of ideas for ways to treat it, and have concluded they're missing a significant piece of the cause as well, despite having identified all of the genes involved in her condition, most of them from the Z chromosome. Not good. A crowdhack is usually a last resort, a prayer to the collective knowledge of the colony. Sometimes the colony answers, sometimes it doesn't.

A message pops up from Rio: *Can't do today. Would be happy to after work tomorrow.*

Sounds great, I write back. *See you then.* I try to sound excited, but any anticipation I feel dissolves into the dread I have for Haruko like a grain of chalk melting in a beaker of acid. Far too little to neutralize.

For the next hour, I offer what I can to the crowdhack, which turns out to be nothing. The doctors have already done everything I can think to do. They still can't find what caused the usually recessive genes in her Z chromosome to suddenly express. Some sudden change at the DNA level caused her body's cells to start making new and different proteins. Her DNA now doesn't match her DNA at birth. Whatever caused it isn't present in her body anymore, but the lack of some catalyst at some past time is a near impossibility. Specialists are scouring her home and work rooms for physical evidence, but the results of that could take days, presuming they actually find something. They've already asked all the right questions. And this is what everyone tells them on the network. The crowdhack is dispersing before it starts.

#

After work I sit in one of the cafeterias to eat dinner, and expand my marble into a network portal to message Hesper and Isaac. Both of them are working late, and I don't blame them. It seems a crime to enjoy oneself while Haruko lies unconscious with unending tests taxing her body further, yet I still feel pulled toward tomorrow. The swim with Rio hovers like a safe haven from the reality of everything else: research shipwide stunted by safety concerns, the usually cheerful faces of strangers in the corridors tainted by my wondering who among them considers herself a victim of Midflight, and on top of it all, Haruko, sedated for days now, possibly dying.

Dying. I have to repeat it in my head before it means anything. Even my great-grandma has yet to die. How can the *Euclid* carry people her age and let people as young as Haruko die?

The image of Raj Ramakrishnan, the oldest colonist aboard, comes to my mind. He talks of engineering the human body to survive on Helena. Yet some of us can't even survive the way we are. How could we ever truly prepare ourselves for life in the unknown?

I ask the network where I can find this man. His location is set on public, no surprise there, and it says he's in one of the domes. As the oldest person aboard, he lived the closest to Midflight. My father has his own understanding of history, my mother has hers. Both are incomplete. And I'm still gathering data, hoping I can somehow put together a version that doesn't shatter my love for this colony. I know better than to ignore the facts, but I'm not willing to take only the word of my parents and a few others two hundred and fifty years removed. Everything I've learned so far might be true, but if I can get closer to the source, then why on burning Io shouldn't I?

I feed my unfinished Portobello sandwich back into the matter reclaimer and hop the nearest maglev, riding through the red-lit arteries of the *Euclid* and wondering, for the first time, which of them lead to her heart.

Seven

The dome no longer holds the chairs that all of us sat in to watch our arrival at Helena. Instead, it's now a low-gravity room, allowing colonists to walk on the inside of the dome's surface and see Helena beneath their feet. How has it been this long since I've looked at her with my own eyes instead of those of satellites? I push off from the floor and float up toward the dome, slowing as I near the center of the space and then gaining back a little speed as I start to fall weakly toward the dome.

I pivot so as to land feet first. I stop softly on the dome's underside. Helena's nightside faces us, her surface aglow with small points of orange light. Volcanoes. I count four visible eruptions. Infrared could tell us how many more hide under cloud cover. How different an environment from the larger continents is this region of the planet, inhospitable instead of allowing what is perhaps a single organism to dominate the entire landmass. I wonder if this view does for Rio what the view of Helena's sunside usually does for me.

I look around the room for the man I came to see, but don't find him at first. Then I see him floating, legs crossed as if he's sitting. Still. How is he doing that when the room has some gravity? Then I get it. He's found the center. He's being pulled weakly in opposite directions by either side of the room. Hesper and I used to play that game as children, trying to jump with just enough strength that we would stop when we reached the middle instead of falling to the other side. Eventually we had our physics teacher formulate it for us, and the specifics were so exact we gave up. You would have to program your skinsuit to move on its own, exert just the right amount of force in just the right direction, and if you breathe, it throws the whole thing off. How did he manage?

I pull out my marble, and turn it into a tether with large knots on each end. I access the dome and make a loop come up out of the transparent surface I stand on, to which I can anchor the tether. I tie it, and carry the rest of the rope with me as I jump up and float toward the center. If I've programmed it correctly, the tether should be just long enough to reach from one end of the room to the other. Anchors at each end will keep it taut enough in the middle that I can hold onto it and climb to within speaking distance of Mr. Ramakrishnan, instead of jumping up and falling back and forth past him over and over again.

It almost works. The tether isn't quite long enough at first, so the second knot, nearly reaching the ground at the "floor" end, just hangs there and bounces clumsily. I toy with the programming and extend the tether just enough to allow each end to touch each surface, anchor the second end to the dome's floor, then climb up it.

Ramakrishnan has been watching me this whole time, but says nothing, merely bows his head.

"I'd like to speak with you," I say.

"Speak," he says. And he's drifting now, the movement of speaking having broken his equilibrium. He'll fall in one direction or the other before long.

"You can share my tether if you don't want to drift," I say. I slip further up so that each of us will be just outside the gravity center, and our weights will pull in opposite directions and balance each other out.

He holds the tether with one hand, and crosses his legs to sit on it.

"How did you get to the center of the room?" I say. "Once I saw the physics of it, it seemed impossible."

"Do you know about baseball?" he says.

"It's an Earth game," I say.

"The pitcher throws the ball. The batter tries to hit it out of the park. To do so is a physics problem equally as complex as jumping to the middle of this room. But the players never look at the numbers. They simply practice until they know how."

"How long did it take you to do it?"

He smiles behind his beard. "I happened across it by accident. I find rooms like this to be useful for exercises in patience. I start with a small jump, barely leaving the ground. Increase little by little. Eventually, I jump all the way to the other side. But the repetition, the constant falling back to the point of origin, is extremely efficient at teaching one to let go of impatience. One day I found myself floating, thinking the fall toward the ceiling or back toward the floor was just slow to start. But as long as I kept still, I never fell. Some days I may try for hours, never quite getting right the jump that will land me, briefly, in the middle. Other times I may float here so long the vitals monitor cuts me short with an order to exercise. But if I do it perfectly, floating is no different than falling up or down, because the goal isn't to float, but to let go of impatience."

"I like zero gravity. I try to stop all momentum and just hang there."

"An equally challenging formula of numbers. But I imagine you don't think of it that way."

"I don't."

"So it is with baseball, and with most things."

I can think of nothing specific to ask about Midflight. I don't know what there is for me to ask. "You've lived a long time."

"A short time, I think."

"What can you tell me about Midflight?"

His crinkled brown face is still. "What are you looking for?"

"I don't know. I feel like this whole ship isn't what I thought. I used to think it was paradise. It was perfect."

"And now?"

"It feels like a mask. Like everyone pretends things are perfect when they're not. Or that nobody really understands that it isn't perfect."

"You want paradise back?"

"Yes."

"You can't get back what never was. All you've lost is your own mask that you didn't realize you were wearing."

"I don't look at people the same anymore. I wonder if everyone is angry underneath."

"Some are. Others have left the past to sort out its own problems."

"I don't know who knows about it and who doesn't. And I can't even know what that time was really like, because everyone who lived back then is gone. Even you weren't born until . . . I don't know, how old are you?"

He laughs. Looks at me with deep, dark eyes. "Old enough to have lived on two different ships. My grandparents were true children of Midflight. They saw their families forsaken by the colony. And strangely enough, you, Edwyn, are a child of Midflight in as true a sense as any. Your parents lived through it."

"My bio-parents, you mean."

"That label is insufficient. They did more than donate their DNA. They made a decision, as parents, to delay your birth until orbit."

"How much do you know about me?"

"As much as you've made public."

"What about my bio-parents? I've looked at their files. There's not much there. I was their only child."

"You were their second child."

"No I wasn't."

"So you've lost your faith in the sincerity of colonists who smile, but you retain your faith in records kept during political turmoil over two hundred years ago."

"I've read every record about them on the network, and there's nothing there about another child."

"Indeed there isn't. Yet I can tell you with certainty that the greatest child of Midflight was their son. He died before my parents were born, but my grandparents knew him."

"What was his name?"

"Guillermo."

I take hold of the rope with both hands, and give Ramakrishnan a pointed look. He smiles, and lets go of the tether. I remotely undo the anchors, and slowly he and I fall in opposite directions, and I coil up the tether, collapse it into a marble. As I land on the clear inside of the dome, I stretch the marble back out into a network portal. Archives. Birth records. Guillermo Santiago. Nothing. Death records, service records, research records, anything. Nothing. I jump off the dome with enough force to propel me to the exit. As I pass Ramakrishnan, who still falls gracefully, I say, "His last name was Santiago?"

"It was."

"If he was ever on this ship, it's been recorded somewhere," I say, calling over my shoulder at him now.

He bows at me as he falls, an awkward contortion, Helena's nightside huge behind him. He says, "Go with grace and dignity."

#

I get off the maglev at the ship's Archival Office, the only place for obscure documents or files that for whatever reason can't be stored on the network. I haven't been here since my Prime School history classes, but I recognize the woman behind the desk as the same one from all those years ago. Short, with red hair, though a little gray now.

"I'm looking for any record of a Guillermo Santiago born around or a little before the Midflight years," I say. The surface of the desk she stands behind is a network portal, so I pull up the profiles of my bio-parents. "These are his parents."

"Sounds familiar," she says. She takes a close look at their profiles. "No children before you," she says. "One thing that doesn't get lost to history on this colony is births."

"He exists, unless that man was sending me on a Snipe hunt."

"A supernova in paralytic entropy is about as nonsensical as an unrecorded birth. But maybe he had different parents."

She does a search on his name.

"I tried that," I say. "All I got was a black hole."

She frowns at her screen, then types it in again. "You may be more right than you know. A black hole is exactly what you found."

"What do you mean?"

"The network hub didn't simply return no results on my search. The search terms themselves never made it to the return stage. Something in the system stopped them from getting there."

"A firewall of some kind?"

"No, that would have given me the no results page. I have a hunch I know who you're looking for. But if I'm right, we won't find a trace of him on the network. Follow me."

We walk past rows of permanent network portals, most of their chairs empty, past a history class like mine where one of the archival experts gives the kids the same talk about the evolution of data storage on the *Euclid*. We keep walking, slide up a zerograv chute to another floor, and enter a room full of computer hardware, shelves of old, boxy, electronic CPUs and monitors, from before DNA data storage, from long before Midflight.

"Ever used one of these?" the woman says.

I shake my head. "I've only seen them in the museum."

"I'll show you how." She sits down at a terminal and starts typing on a keyboard that has real, three-dimensional keys. "Every once in a while, data on the network can be corrupted or erased, despite our backup systems and recovery tools and genuinely ingenious technicians. When I say once in a while, I mean once in a hundred years. We started keeping fully electronic, un-networked backups of vital data like birth records around Midflight. And the reason for it was, I believe, a certain amount of data damage possibly done by the man you're researching, if indeed it's who I'm thinking of."

"What did he do?"

"It may not have been him necessarily. Historians haven't been able to determine if he was the cause or simply the victim. That is, whether he tried to erase his own records or someone else did."

"What's the point of that? Can't people just make new records? Or reconstruct the old ones?"

"That became exponentially harder because at the same time his records were destroyed, he died. It was far from coincidental. Suicide or murder, one of the two."

"Wait, we're talking about Midflight, not pre-collaborative-era Earth, right? People have been killed on this ship?"

"Possibly. As I said, no one's entirely sure what happened. The only way to reconstruct records was to talk to people who knew him. And if any of them weren't truthful, there's no way to know."

"You mean he erased everything? Even surveillance?"

"Someone wrote a virus that operated a lot like the facial recognition software that the surveillance cameras use. It destroyed every file, every recording, every image, piece of text, what have you, that was tagged with his digital signature. All of the research papers with his name on them, all of the video files he happens to appear in, even incidentally. Everything."

"So what's on these old computers?"

"The little data that's been reconstructed. Records detailing the investigation into his death. They tried making new files on the network, but every time the file would get eaten, essentially, by the virus. Whoever wrote the program did such a good job that two hundred years later, it's still there, hiding buried in the network. That's why I didn't even get a no-results return on my search. The only way to retain any information about him is to do so on a computer not connected to the network. And the only ones on the ship that never connect, that can't connect, are right in front of you. Why don't you have a seat."

She stands up. I take her place in the chair. "This is him?"

"Everything we know about him."

"Thank you," I say to her. "You're amazing."

"It's what I do. And no offense to your parents' dignity, but I think there are definite drawbacks to having your children born centuries after you. It makes learning about your bio-relatives much more frustrating."

"I've never met anyone besides me whose parents did that."

She smiles, but with a bitter note. "Why else do you think I would work in a place like this?"

Then she leaves.

I look at my brother's face, or rather two reconstructions of it: an artist's and a computer's. The computer's version looks empty, emotionless. The artist's looks similar, the work of someone who didn't know him, working from descriptions given by people who did. Guillermo Santiago. Who were you?

I page through the records, the operating system of these old computers being fairly intuitive. At the far end of the room, a young man sits at a table cleaning the inside of one of these CPUs, replacing worn-out components with care. Everything so fragile, with none of the elasticity or transformative properties I grew up accustomed to. I have to stop myself from trying to stretch the screen out so I can work in a larger space.

My bio-parents said of Guillermo that he almost never left his lab. He even applied for a special exemption from parent duty so that he could more fully commit himself to his research: bioengineering.

My stomach does a back flip. Can it be a coincidence? My mother has never mentioned knowing that my bio-parents had another child. But Ramakrishnan knew. And she loves to hear him speak. I can barely handle reading any more, but can't stop myself. He was working on a way to adapt humans to the atmosphere of Helena.

My mother definitely knew. Did she know before she decided to be my mother? Did she decide to be *my* mother because I am Guillermo's sister? What about my father? I can't imagine him lying to me, and I refuse to accept that he could have. He never encouraged me to study bioengineering. That was all Mom. What did she want?

Guillermo's lab was found sterile and empty. Someone had reprogrammed the walls, illegally, into a giant matter disassembler. All of his research, and Guillermo himself, was broken into atoms and sent to bulk matter storage. From there his atoms—carbon, hydrogen, oxygen—went every which way, assembled into clothes, tools, food, perhaps even a component for one of these computers that holds all that's left of him. The same day, all files on the network that connected to him disappeared. As far as the network was concerned, he'd never been born. The room he worked in was never his lab, the people who knew him had imagined him.

Enough people had met him, had co-authored papers with him, had visited his lab with questions for him, that bits and pieces of his research were reconstructed, but his equations, his designs, his innovative molecules, all had to be recreated from memory, and very little was salvaged. The only things remaining that were possibly his work were the room-sized disassembler and the computer virus.

Colleagues of his said he was not interested in computers. His parents said he didn't mind them. Murder or suicide, no one could say. But you can't turn a room into a disassembler by accident, and you can't circumvent the ship's safety programming without complex orchestration.

People unrelated to him but who knew of his death called it murder: an anti-colonization hate crime to prevent a bioengineering solution to settling on Helena. Another crime against dignity just like the referendums. This kept the investigation going for months, but no enemies were found and in the end no one could rule out suicide. Reports were released in hard copy after being written up on computers like the one I sit using. In time, the investigation was stopped after they had run out of leads. Technicians tried in vain to remove the virus from the network. Eventually, they too gave up.

Here official records stop, and the work of historians steps in, work that, by virtue of containing his name, can never be posted on the network without instant erasure. By the time fifty years had passed, his death had become a legend the network couldn't verify. A hundred years after his death, hard copies forgotten, it was an oral tradition passed down by the Children of Midflight, an apocryphal story of a martyr. Whether he was murdered or driven to suicide made little difference; both could be seen as the effect of the majority strangling away the minority's hope of release from a ship many had come to see as a prison. The Children of Midflight saw colonization as the embodiment of all they had been denied when the *Euclid* gave them no way to return to Earth. Why had the ship left Io to begin with but to find a new place to live under an open sky?

Ramakrishnan called Guillermo "the greatest" child of Midflight. He said his own grandparents knew him. Despite that so many years separate us from Midflight, the chain that connects us to it needs very few links. Is this how wounds two centuries old can still feel fresh in a gathering like the Children of Midflight? Is this how my mother can see me as a child of Midflight myself before I am even conceived from the archived spawn of my bio-parents?

I have learned enough. I close the various documents, log out of the archaic computer, and head toward the exit, toward home, toward my mother.

Eight

The corridor outside my home has gone dark, and the façade of stars and moonlit clouds on the ceiling strikes me as insufferably fake. I stand in front of the doors, keeping my breaths measured but unable to calm myself. I push the panel to open the doors. My parents sit at a wooden picnic table, the floor set on fake grass with the walls showing rendered trees, false mountains, and a projected sunset. My mother and father look at me.

"Can you turn this burning fantasy off?" I say.

"What's wrong?" My mother says, standing up.

"Turn it off." I look her in the eye, and she knows I'm serious.

She looks at my father, and he plays with a few buttons on the table. The walls clear, the floor turns to carpet, the room reverted to the way it really is, gray and bare and empty but for the picnic table, which stands out sorely.

My mother crosses her arms. "I don't appreciate your rudeness."

Words fly by in my mind. How to fit everything I feel and know into a single statement?

It can't be done. All I can say is, "How could you?"

My mother's face softens, slightly, but her body remains posed, stern. "How could I what?"

I can't even speak again. The anger turns to despair, and my knees shake, and the rest of my body trembles with them. I lower myself to the floor, the tears flowing now. "Nothing's real anymore," I say, slurring my words.

My mother crouches in front of me, and my father appears beside her, carefully getting down on his own knees. "It's all right, Edwyn," he says. "You're safe."

I manage to look at each of them. Their faces concerned, not angry, caring. I can't look at them anymore. The small comfort they try to give morphs the despair back into anger. The words come.

"Why did you lie to me? Why couldn't you tell me?"

My mother's voice is no longer steady: "What, Edwyn? Tell you what?"

"Everything."

I know that's the least helpful answer to give but don't care. They should know. And that jab, that accusation that they have been making my whole life a lie, gives me the strength to say his name to their faces. "About Guillermo."

They are silent. I have to look away again.

"You wanted me to be him. You wanted me to be . . ." I force the words out, ". . . not me."

Their inability to speak and to deny tells me that somewhere in what I have just accused them of, there is a piece of the truth.

"That's not fair," my mother says. She sounds hurt. "That's not true."

The hurt in her voice blunts the weakness I feel. It satisfies me. I look her in the eye now, look at her wounded expression, and say, fully intending to offend her dignity, "Burn on Io."

Then I stand. My father stands as if to catch hold of me, and I turn and hurry from the room, my mother letting go of a single sob before the doors cut her off. I run to the maglev station and hop in, pick the furthest destination I can think of, the far end of the ship, and within the tight walls of the pod I let out the rest of my rage and grief, my childish noises resounding as I shoot through the tunnels of the only thing that has yet to betray my trust: the *Euclid* herself.

#

I am still traveling through the dark and red when I come back to my body. I feel as if I have shed my skin like a snake or a cicada, and that I had to look the Law of Dignity in the eye and break it before I could cast off my old self. My mother, if she chooses, could report my violation of the verbal abuse clause. I would be unable to deny it. The furious spike in my vital signs has probably already been sent to my counselor, who may even be waiting for me when I reach my destination, carrying a lecture on constructive outlets for anger. If so, I will not talk. I have nothing to say.

The burden of explanation rests on my mother and father now. They must have known about Guillermo before they chose to be the parents of me in particular. Did they have to compete with others for the privilege? Did all of the Children of Midflight want to raise the sibling of Guillermo? It sounds silly and melodramatic even as I think it, but no more believable scenario comes to my mind.

The maglev stops. I disembark and look around the station to see if anyone waits for me. The station is empty. Should I be relieved or worried? I go out into the corridor, not sure exactly where I am. Somewhere in the Upper Stern quadrant. I touch the corridor wall and open a network portal. I'm on a mostly residential deck, but not far from the Upper Stern Park. I memorize the route there and set off, surprised at how, even though the corridors look the same, the place feels unfamiliar. How little of the ship do I confine myself to by following the same routine every day? Are there places on the ship I've never been?

I find the door to the park and it displays a warning: protective gear required when walking or climbing outside marked paths. I set my skinsuit on Fall Protection, a motion-sensing getup that can inflate instantaneously to prevent climbing injuries. Somewhere in my memory, I know what's behind this door, but it's been too many years, and I've filled my head with too much other information to see it clearly. I walk through.

It's a dome—the largest on the ship, I remember now, having seen it on schematics many a time. And in it lies a mountain, or a mountaintop, by Earth standards. A gray stone peak surrounded by pines at its base. I walk down the path, a red-brown carpet of needles crunching softly underfoot, and everything comes back to me, from my Prime School geography classes to a camping trip. When did I go on a camping trip? I must have been only two or three years old. Mom and Dad and I came here, and we followed the steps to the top of the mountain, but I barely remember what we did, what I felt. I don't know what's different or what's the same. Between the dark pine trunks, I see distant lights in the woods, camps like ours. The stars overhead shine brilliantly, a star map with no constellations yet, but with enough constancy over the past few years that I can still find where Earth's sun hides if I look long enough.

I follow the foot-beaten trail to the base of the mountain, a ten-minute walk if I move leisurely. The ground rises, and rocky outcroppings split the rug of needles, jutting up in waves until they link together, so numerous now that the forest thins, becomes a lone tree here, a shrub there. It's barely a kilometer to the summit, the laws of physics preventing keeping an actual mountain on the ship. I remember from geography that all this is fake underneath, the rocks real, leftovers from a mine on the Ganymede colony, but under the mountain lies an enormous artificial cavern with well-placed supports. The rock under my feet extends only a dozen meters down before it opens into air. But none of that is visible from here, the cavern accessible only from an entrance on the far end of the dome, or from the deck below this one. The illusion is convincing.

The steps grow steep. I have gym lectures to thank for not losing my breath, but I haven't used a staircase this long in years. I imagine that somewhere hidden on the slopes, off the path, lovers climb to nooks and hollows to hide away. Probably not what Rio would be interested in, if we were ever to become more than friends, but then again, do I really know khen well enough to say what khe'd like? I don't. We're still planning to swim tomorrow.

My mother's faces, angry and then stricken, come back, but my legs and lungs work too hard right now to let my emotions curl me up. I climb more quickly, and though her image stays, I can let it.

I stop at the sound of a deep, hollow, resounding beat of a drum. It must be the size of a person to resound for so long. Another beat, and I feel the vibration in my bones. Not a drum but a gong, played gently to accentuate the lower tones. It comes from up, from the summit. I climb in step with it, every eight stairs another echo of this endlessly low-pitched sound. After eight beats, a second drum joins, not quite so deep, a concert bass perhaps, two quick beats following the gong, then five beats of silence. A drum circle? When I joined with Choir, I looked at all the professional music groups on the network, but this wasn't listed. Maybe it's just a group of friends playing. Maybe I would be intruding.

A third drum now, timpani by the sound of it. And a fourth, bongos, the rhythm complicating every time a new voice joins. By the time I reach the summit, the sound has texture, depth, a mix of high, middle, and low percussion, the rhythm so long and complex it takes the full eight beats to play out. I take the last few steps up and see the circle of drummers, a small dome in the middle of them with a convincing projection of a campfire inside. The drummers play with their eyes closed, and beyond them the summit overlooks the entire park. The treetops stand far below, the dome's circular base beyond them, and outside it I can see clear to the far end of the *Euclid*, her dimly lit white hull stretching to its own horizon, smaller domes visible further along, and beyond that, the black of space and the field of stars, the slim crescent of Helena's atmosphere nearly hidden behind the ship, our ship, our colony. The sight brings back the sadness I thought I had left in the maglev. I hug myself looking out at the vast expanse of my home.

Behind me, the voices in the drum circle fall silent one by one. They must have noticed me. I pull myself together before I turn around to face them.

They all are staring at me, and when I meet their eyes, they stand in unison and bow. Only with their drums out of the way do I realize they're all wearing Operations uniforms, a bridge that links them across their varied ages and ranks, and which feels oddly like it separates them from me.

A short man with very Japanese features says, "Good evening."

I stumble over the words, belying my appearance of composure. "Good evening."

"I must ask if you're an adult."

"I am."

"Then welcome. Regulation requires that I disclose the religious nature of this ceremony. You are free to stay or leave as you wish."

They look at me expectantly.

It's still difficult to speak. "I'm sorry. I didn't mean to interrupt."

"Do you wish to participate? The circle is open." His eyes shine in the firelight, his kindly, unjudging gaze reaching clear into my still tender hurt. He says, "We drum because we are human, and something within us, some spirit, some yearning, draws us to. We use it to cast away our discontented layers, to connect with a part of us that remains constant. The rhythm of drumming opens the door to a trance where only a contented self remains. There, we heal ourselves and strengthen our care for others."

I find nothing to say in response. I change the subject. "You're all in Operations."

He smiles, and looks around the circle. "Running the ship is hierarchical. Some of us benefit from reminding ourselves we're all the same."

I look at their faces, old and young, men and women, technicians and crew chiefs, all of their eyes glinting. I think of my cousin in Operations and vaguely wonder whether she knows of this.

"Take my drum," the man says. "Sit." His tone is gentle, so much that I cannot refuse his offer. I walk around the circle to him, and he steps aside to let me into his chair. Everyone sits at once.

The drums are arranged in the order I heard them start, the gong next to the bass, and so on until the highest instrument, something like a tambourine, completes the circle. Everyone places their hands, ready to play, and closes their eyes. A woman not quite my mother's age, black hair pulled back, uniform crisp and ready for duty, raises her soft mallet and gently strikes the gong once, twice, three times, a faster rhythm than before, but the sound the same long, dark timbre, like the music of a singing black hole. The bass drum joins, and makes clear this rhythm is in threes instead of fours, a steady strike on every beat. The timpani extends the rhythm to six beats instead of three, alternating its rhythm between two different phrases.

By the time the circle gets to me, with my ethnic drum I have no name for, I can only manage a single beat, in time with the gong, alternating which hand I play it with. But even with such a small contribution, I feel myself fading into the larger whole, the sound surrounding me and resounding inside me, a feeling I haven't felt since the last time I sang with Choir, a good month now.

So many things have changed since then.

Helena. Haruko. Rio. Pam. Guillermo. My mother.

I close my eyes like the other drummers do. The drumming keeps the wandering parts of my mind busy with counting beats, with moving my hands, and though I still feel the swell of sadness in my breastbone, my hands striking the hard, stretched fabric of the drum channel something out, or maybe in.

When the last drummer enters the rhythm, the woman at the gong changes her steady downbeat strike, switching to the second, fourth, and sixth beats to swing her mallet. One by one, the other instruments follow suit, changing their rhythm to some other rhythm, and the sound of all of us morphs, over the course of some minutes, into a totally different sound. The faces, the truths I have learned, the losses I have felt, extend from my chest down into my hands, and when my turn comes to change, I pick up the pace: right-left-left, right-left-left, right. Right-left-left, right-left-left, right.

It takes all of my concentration to keep this going, and the constant, complicated sounds of all those around me fill my body like water. The next time I notice anything but the drums inside me and out, the feeling of fabric on my hands, I do not know how long it has been, how many times the rhythm has circled through us. I know only that the gong has stopped. The bass has stopped. The timpani. The bongos. And then my hands and arms, too, go limp and numb. There is nothing left inside me but clear, open space, as if I have evaporated into the universe and become the black on which the stars are hung.

Nine

After repeatedly thanking the members of the drum circle and finding a public-use room to set on private and spend the night, I wake up to a message from Rio blinking on my bed's network portal, two hours before I planned to wake up. It says, "Something came up for tonight. Want to go swimming now instead? Lower Stern Pool. I'm already there."

My arms feel tired and sore from the night before, but I have slept so deeply that I don't remember any dreams. Arms aside, my body feels rested despite the early waking. I touch the screen and message back, "Sure. Be there in ten minutes." I get out of bed, pull myself together, and flip through my clothes settings for a wetsuit.

A quick maglev ride takes me to the Lower Stern Pool, which I've never seen empty no matter the hour, though this early there are maybe four people in the fifty-meter pool. I remove my shoes from my wetsuit and sit down on the cold tile at the edge. The water's warm.

I look for Rio among the swimmers, and see khen surface at the far end, notice me, then turn around and dive back in. Khe swims toward me with visible ease, smooth movement, good technique. I swim for fun more than for anything else, and haven't practiced technique since Prime School. Khe reaches my end, and holds onto the edge next to me. Khes shoulders are visibly toned, but narrow for someone who otherwise looks male. The close proximity of our bodies in the thick humidity stirs a certain primal, immature curiosity about khes body, but

I keep it at bay. The questions I might ask are shallow, silly even—I know I'm attracted to whatever body khe has, whether it be closer to male, female, or somewhere squarely in between. I don't need the details. After the cathartic numbness of the night before, I'm just using khes body as an excuse not to focus on the one piece of myself left resounding in the back of my mind: the words I said to my mother.

Khe says, "Want to come in?"

"I don't know. I had . . ." What can I say about last night? A religious experience? I don't know if that's accurate or not. "I exercised my arms a lot yesterday. They're still tired."

"Okay. I've done my laps already. We can just tread in the shallows if you want."

"That sounds good." I push off and sink into the water, let the warmth slide up me, over my face, before I float back up so my head's in the open air. We swim along the short end of the pool, ducking under the ropes that divide the lanes, until we get to the shallows on the far side.

"I've heard some talk," Rio says, "about the scanners coming online today. Word is the background radiation levels are high enough for most of what we were hoping to use."

Helena. It feels like a week since I was in the simulator yesterday. "That's pretty exciting," I say, without feeling a word of it. There's too much else. Midflight, Guillermo, my parents, everything.

"I've seen your lab reports," Rio says. "This should answer a lot of questions, right?"

Here khe is, trying to make decent conversation, and here I am uninterested. "More likely to raise questions than answer them, I think," I say, and the thought of working with Pam again today does manage to make me smile. "If our work so far is any indication."

"It should help us to confirm a lot of what we think we're seeing in geology," khe says. "If we're right, we might have a possible location for a bubble colony, like the ones back near Earth. A young island, volcanically formed. Inactive. No plants, no wildlife yet, just rock. We could observe the life on Helena while remaining isolated from it, having a negligible effect on its biosphere."

There's a rare enthusiasm in khes voice, and the weight of what khe's saying hits me.

"But there's so much history," I say, moving my arms and legs to keep afloat. "So many people who want to be a real part of that biosphere. Didn't we leave Io in the first place because we were isolated?"

Rio shrugs in the water. "I think to most of the colonists, a large number anyway, history is history. The people who left Io are all long gone.

"What about Midflight?"

"What about it?"

Khens is a genuine question. Is Midflight not the lurking discontent in the colony that I thought it was? Is the Children of Midflight just a fringe group? Does no one else know the real story? Surely people couldn't know it and not care.

"Most people, I think," Rio says, "will be happy just to have a place to explore outside the ship. Real sky. A real sun. Real ground to walk on. What people wanted above Io, I think, is Earth. What did they want during Midflight? Earth. That's the history we can't escape. Not Io."

"You sound a bit like my father," I say, and feel that swell of sadness again, wishing for the family I had before yesterday, the one I trusted.

"I've met him," Rio says. "I think highly of him."

"You do? Have you said anything to him about me?"

Rio laughs. "Like what?"

"I . . . don't know. That you met me?"

"I don't think I've seen him since I met you. Not in a few weeks, anyway."

I chew on that. Has khe met everyone in my life before? First Haruko, now my father.

"Haruko," I say, finally. I've been unable to even think about her. Unable to go see her again for fear things have only gotten worse.

"I'm seeing her tonight. After work," Rio says. Khe pauses. "They're saying her body is weakening under the stress. That's why I got up early to swim now instead. So tonight I can visit."

I stop moving and start to sink, grab the edge of the pool to steady myself. "Can I come with you?"

Khe nods. "That would be nice."

"Thank you," I say, though it's clear khe's just as upset about this as I am. I grab the edge of the pool with both hands now, put my cheek to the warm, wet concrete wall just above the water, close my eyes. "I don't want to lose her."

Rio's close to me now. I can feel khes body in the water next to mine.

"I know," khe says, and under the water khe touches my shoulder. I take one hand from the wall and hold Rio's.

We are suspended in silence but for the echoes of the water rippling against us, the distant splash of a diver at the far end plunging through the surface.

#

I eat a nutrition bar in the corridor on the way to Pam's lab, and before I get there I hear the people passing me whispering to each other as the corridor sky begins to lighten. Today, after seeing Haruko, I must make a point to see Hesper or Isaac no matter how late they work, even if it means going to their labs in person to see what's going on. People hurry like it's Orbit Day all over again, and I find myself quickening my pace to see what's happening.

Pam sits at her workstation in the lab, early as usual, to the point I have to doubt whether she ever goes home at night.

"I haven't been on the network yet," I say. "What's the news?"

"Multiple planetary scans in progress," she says. "Results so far are indicating a much lower level of complexity in marine life than was estimated, but it's still turning everything we know about anaerobic evolution and anoxygenic complexity on its head. But Helena is hundreds of millions of years older than Earth, and has had much more time without oxygen for evolution to play with. Today is the day everyone in the bio labs has been waiting for. By the end of the scans, we'll have enough data to last a year before we do it again, though I'm sure we'll do another one the same time tomorrow."

"What about the plant life?"

"Interesting question. It turns out our friend the continent-sized organism is, so far, just that. Scans have only just reached the continent we're looking at. But look at these images." She shows me various data on the screen, pointing to a translucent 3D model of the forest floor thus far. "All of the trunks, nodes, everything, grow from this same root system, and it's beginning to look more like a larger version of the structure of Earth fungi, with threadlike hyphae or something like them connecting into systems like subterranean mycelium. And fungi, I should point out, are more closely related to animals than plants, at least along Earth's evolutionary tree. Obviously we're looking at a more outwardly plantlike system, but the ways in which its various 'trees' are connected are starting to form a much different picture. The changes in color we saw are still a mystery, but in another couple hours that may change."

"Can we feed this data stream into the simulator?"

"All of it? That might be counterproductive. It's a composite of about ten different scans."

"I want to try."

"Be my guest."

I put on the headgear, adjust my skinsuit's gloves, step onto the platform, and in the simulation surround myself with various windows showing the feed from the different scanners. In them, I isolate the plant system we've been studying, and pull out each scan's version of it, infrared, backscatter, all of it except for the satellite visual. I expand all of the data until I have a 3D image around me not of how the plant system looks visually, but of its internal structure, and I overlay these various scans until they combine into a single map, each translucent and identifiable by color. I stand in a forest of bright greens, blues, reds, yellows against a background of black for maximum visibility.

I reach out and scale the image down, taking in what I'm seeing at the "tree" level and keeping it in mind while I shrink the image and rotate it as if I'm looking down from a thousand feet in the air.

"Am I seeing an electric field?" I ask Pam.

"A weak one, yes. There are electrochemical actions happening, most of them subterranean."

I stretch the image back out, expanding it now, zeroing in on the top of the root mountain I climbed to yesterday, bringing myself into one of the nublike leaves atop the highest branch, expanding it until I can see its cellular structure. It's a mix of things that trigger disparate memories from bio classes, eight or nine distinct cell types that I can't identify from memory, but that I tag for later study. I follow the branch down into the trunk, into the subterranean root system, and see a highly stratified set of differently dense root types. Some reach deep into the ground like ordinary plant roots. Others come down one trunk and twist into a coil with hundreds of others, connecting to one or to a thousand other trunks, winding together into great knots. I shrink the image again and try to trace the root paths visually.

"The integration here is incredible," I say. "There must be billions of connections between the various trunks. What would one tree get from being connected to another a thousand miles away?"

"Wrong question," Pam says. "What would one organism get from having a highly-integrated surface area of thousands of square miles?"

"A lot of solar energy," I say. "A lot of nutrients from the ground. All that seems straightforward. But the connections here are so complex. It could be for energy sharing, maybe, allowing a weaker trunk to get help from a stronger one."

"It wouldn't surprise me at all, but my gut tells me there are a thousand things happening at once here. I like to familiarize myself with the components individually before seeing how they work together."

"I'm the opposite," I say. "I think the big picture tells us where to start in understanding the individual components."

"That's true for complex life of the highest order," Pam says.

A moment of silence passes.

She says, "Is that what you think we're seeing?"

"I'm not making that call yet," I say. "Is there a way to see, visually, the electrochemical activity?"

"Easy enough. But the data suggest you'd be seeing flashes too quick for the eye to follow. I can't recommend it."

"Slow it down," I say. "I want to see what's happening here."

"Give me a minute," Pam says. "You're asking for a hugely customized visualization."

I take a moment to orient myself again, rotating the image so that I see the root mountain at a three-quarter angle from below, the web of forest tendrils spreading to its own horizon in every direction. I switch off all of the data except the red and green hues that mark the root structure and stratification of root types.

"Here's your visual," Pam says.

The root mountain lights up, so brilliantly I can no longer discern the red and green. White light flows through every branch, trunk, coil of twisted underground cable. I can't even speak at first. "Pam, you need to see this," I say.

"I see it."

I stretch the image out, zooming in until the roots surround me, the central coil of enormous knots at the base of the mountain engulfed in so much movement of light I can barely stand to look at it. I move it aside, look more closely at the outer edges, where the knots disentangle into complex coils that web out and connect every tree to every other. Here, where the light is less dense, I can get a handle on what's happening. Flashes of light travel out and in, this way and that along the twisted coils, concentrated there, but branching out into everything else, even the roots that dig for water in the bedrock.

"Correct me if I'm wrong," I say, "but doesn't this look an awful lot like synaptic activity in a nervous system?"

Pam is silent. I watch the signals until I get dizzy.

"You're not wrong," she says. "But a nervous system on a scale this size is unprecedented. Nervous systems govern behavior, which I'm not sure an organism of this size can be said to have. Unless we're looking at a likewise unprecedentedly slow time scale." I can almost hear her nod. "Which, for an organism of this size, would make perfect sense."

I can't contain a little jump. And then another. "This complexity, this activity," I say. "Doesn't this alone warrant a lab report?"

"Ordinarily I'd say not to count your supernovae before they collapse. But yes, in this case, the data are enough to warrant the attention of everyone."

"I want to write it."

"Go ahead. But I may need to add some things, and make sure your conclusions are appropriate. Despite everything we just said to each other, we're ages away from conclusive evidence that we've just seen the largest, slowest brain ever discovered."

"Sounds like a deal." I pull off the headset. "And I caught you. You just had to spell out precisely what we didn't just discover."

"What can I say," Pam says, smiling at me from her workstation, her crow's feet and smile wrinkles spreading farther than ever. "Sometimes the thrill of possibility gets hold of even me. And if you can muster that much enthusiasm for writing a lab report every day, you can bet I'll keep you in my lab as long as I can."

"If we keep having this much fun, you won't have to try very hard." I sit down at my own workstation, pull up the data stream, and start writing. Even the mundane, technical language of the report can't put a dent in the excitement of what we've just seen: the possibility of a consciousness the size of a continent.

If this turns out to be what it looks like, the Law of Dignity will rule out any possibility of terraforming. I try not to think about the trouble that might cause. All the more reason to get extra eyes on the data.

#

I sit laboring over the meticulously uncertain wording of the report's "conclusions" section when the ship's quarantine alarm goes off. Red lights, alerts on our monitors, unmistakable. Pam and I stand up from our chairs and expand our marbles into personal containment pods. We step in. The inside surface shows the details of the outbreak, symptoms of the disease, and people now known to have contracted it.

The image shows the greenish, broken skin I've seen on Haruko. Next to her face on the carrier list are two more cases admitted to the hospital deck, both people in the age group of Haruko and me.

Ten

The various screens on the inside of my pod flash live updates from the med team working on Haruko and now on these two other kids. I turn the volume down until I can hear myself think. They work to isolate the pathogen, to determine if it's airborne, and to see who, if anyone, might have immunity. Outside our pods, the *Euclid*'s air purification system works on its highest setting, so much that the strap of the sim goggles hanging off the desk blows back and forth in the wind. I scroll through the written information streaming onto the network from the med team and from other experts trapped in their pods in their own labs.

With so many eyes on the data and on the blood samples, outbreaks like this usually get cleared up in an hour or two. But until now, they didn't think Haruko's condition was in the least way communicable. Already the responses and insights from the shipwide attention to the issue start piling up on yet another screen.

I look over to Pam. She's programmed a stool to sit on inside her pod, and she stares into the data with arms crossed, forehead furrowed, eyes scanning back and forth, her graying hair so still it could quiver with her heartbeat. I dare not disturb her. I scan through the updates and crowd-assigned tasks, looking for something I can do. The blood samples look very odd, with what could be hundreds of unusual cells mixed in. No wonder they haven't been able to pinpoint the culprit yet. All of the Z-chromosome genes that this virus suddenly causes to be expressed are doing a good job covering the tracks of the original contaminant. But with thousands of people looking at this, it shouldn't take long.

When Haruko went into critical condition, there wasn't a trace of a virus, except, of course, for the altered DNA; by itself not conclusive evidence of a pathogen. Something in these new carriers must have suggested the virus was still present in them. It shouldn't be much longer until they narrow it down to only a few suspects.

As I watch, the unusual cells in the blood samples get labeled type by type as innocuous. It starts out quickly, and the list dwindles. Ten possibilities. Eight. Seven. Things slow down. The last few get checked against the air purification system. No matches. It isn't airborne.

I breathe out, just now feeling how tense my body has become. Surveillance records show that Haruko had no direct contact with the other two patients since she contracted the condition, but once we start going back months, things get fuzzier. A virus with that long of a gestation period before affecting the host is harder to track. Maybe it was spread by a third party, a carrier, who came in contact with all three of them? The crowd is ahead of me on that possibility, and already using the network to comb for possible third parties.

While all this goes on, a window pops up with an important development: since all of the difficulties associated with virus result from it causing sudden expression of the Z chromosome, people without a Z are likely immune. Because my bio-parents lived so long ago, I don't have one. This gives me first a thrill of relief, then a sick feeling in my gut. Hesper has a Z. My father has a Z. And if I'm immune, I could theoretically be a carrier. How many people did Haruko touch back when she thought it was an isolated genetic condition, not a virus? I lean against the back wall of my pod.

Data from some quick lab experiments comes through. They've positively identified the pathogen. Once they figure out how it's transmitted, containment crews will come around and take a blood sample from each of the population to determine who needs to be quarantined. Now we're getting somewhere. I stand up straight and watch the data come in.

Definitely transmittable through blood transfusion, but none of the patients received or gave blood in the past year. The patients' saliva is clean. Sweat is clean. Sexual transmission is possible, but surveillance suggests none of the patients knew each other or had any sexual contact. In my mind this means there has to be an immune carrier, or several.

Doctors are questioning the two newer patients on their sexual histories now. They've ruled out enough methods of transmission to relax the level of containment, though, and so we're now allowed to leave our pods, provided we wear sterilizing skinsuits that cover all but our heads, that we avoid direct contact with anyone but the med staff, and that we stay within our current rooms until the entire population has been tested for the virus.

I open my pod, step out, and collapse it into a marble. Pam stays inside hers, still watching the data. I pace around the lab, absently organizing the desk, putting the goggles back into their locker. I sit at the console where I was writing the lab report on Helena, close those files, and expand the emergency screen. No new methods of transmission discovered yet. If it's sexual or blood transmission only, I should be clean, unless the virus has a gestation period of over two years. I dated a little my first couple years of Path, but haven't had sex with anyone since then.

It isn't long before a man in a full body containment suit comes in with a hovering rack of blood samples in tow. Pam looks up at last from the data and steps out of her pod. The man scans my ID and takes a blood sample from my finger and waits for his handheld device to bring the result.

"You've got it," he says, without looking up. "Do you have a Z chromosome?"

"No."

He marks the sample with my ID number and a tag that says "NO Z." He stashes it in the rack.

He takes Pam's sample. "Positive. Do you have a Z?"

"Yes."

"Your vitals will be monitored through the network. First sign of any symptoms, report to the hospital deck."

"How many people have you tested?" I ask.

He puts Pam's sample in the rack. "All together, the team's gotten four hundred in the past fifteen minutes."

"And?"

"All positive. A hundred percent." He leaves the room.

I look at Pam. "All positive? That can't be."

"There's another method of transmission. Has to be."

"Two-thirds of the ship has a Z."

She gets back into her pod, but leaves the door open. "The results are on the network. Four hundred forty and counting."

"There's no way everyone on the ship has it," I say. "Not unless it's in the air."

"It's not in the air. The purifier would have caught it a long time ago."

"In the food?"

"People looking into that. But no organic molecule survives the disassembler. Assembled food should be pure."

"No organic molecule," I repeat. "What's organic that not a single person on the ship can avoid? Only other people, right? Or something in the Deck One Park. We were all there on Orbit Day."

"It wouldn't have to be all organic," Pam says. She removes her hands from the keyboard she has in front of her. "A piece of technology with organic components could in theory be a carrier."

I have my arms crossed, but they go limp and fall to my sides. "You can't mean the network."

"I can. If we think of the ship as an ecosystem, the one resource everyone uses besides air, heat, shelter, and reassembled food and water is the central network hub. Individual workstations like this should be fine because they're isolated: they connect to the hub wirelessly. But everybody sometimes stops to use a console in the corridor. And those are all hard-wired to the hub with both electric and organic components."

"So the original carrier infected the network, then. I mean, it couldn't have originated there."

"Not likely, no."

"Are you putting all this on the network?"

"Already done."

"Has anyone tested it?"

"Coming in now."

I step over to her pod and lean in to look over her shoulder at the screen. An image appears of a virus cell living on what I recognize as one of the polymer-organic-hybrid screen membranes.

Pam says, "Every time you plug one of your marbles into a corridor port for wired access, that's akin to sexual transmission on the technological level. And if that's one of your clothing marbles, you're going to get it pretty quick."

"Burning Io."

"It's worse than Io," Pam says. "If we don't find a cure, we're looking at two thirds of this colony exhibiting symptoms. And if Ms. Kanno's case is any indication, that means two thirds eventually in critical condition. Or worse."

"Gene re-sequencing," I say. "Remove the Z chromosome from everyone's genome."

"That would take months, even if the whole ship worked day and night at it. We need a way to kill this thing."

"Or survive it."

"If you want to go back into bioengineering, now would be the time. I won't hold it against you."

My mother's face again. I ignore it. "I'm going into the simulator," I say.

"What for?"

"I need a closer look at how this thing works."

I take out the goggles and change my skinsuit's gloves, and step onto the platform.

I'm still on Helena, watching the synaptic activity of this primeval, continent-sized organism we're only just beginning to understand. Maybe it and the virus are not so different, conquering everything in their paths, spreading unchecked.

I disconnect the satellite uplink and go into the network, throwing data this way and that, stashing important lab reports in small icons at my feet. The tens of thousands of people online have already organized the project into several major categories: charting the virus's life-cycle and specific effects in order to boost host survival, and mapping its genome to aid the creation of antibodies. Not yet ready to jump into either of those, I clear away everything except a 3D model of a virus cell. I expand it until it's as tall as I am, turn it around, take in its structure, then expand it even more until I can explore it on the inside, uncover its hidden complexities and flaws.

Various parts of its genome appear in real time as they're mapped and identified. All of its major components float around me with only a few small gaps that fill in as I watch. I switch to the life-cycle node of the crowdhack, and watch the virus attach itself to cells of all kinds. It's unbelievable how many types of places it attaches, penetrates a cell, and uses the cell to produce new copies of itself. This is only half the story, though. It inserts its own DNA into the host cell, affecting which proteins that cell manufactures for the host's body. In humans with a Z, the "junk DNA" in the Z chromosome, with its usually unexpressed genes, suddenly gets manufactured by the cell, resulting in the expression of those genes: the skin mutations and terrible shock to the body that threaten to kill Haruko and now these two new patients. I watch this play out over and over in the 3D simulation. It's so burning efficient.

I collapse the life-cycle node and switch over to the host effects node. The skin mutations express a lot of different genes from the Z chromosome, and some of the chemicals and proteins they produce look startlingly like molecules I've seen before but can't place. They don't look like the human proteins I've learned so well, and I haven't had a non-human-focused microbiology class since a year or two ago. But I pick one molecule in particular, one I'm sure I've seen, and throw it into a database window, instructing the computer to see if any known molecules match its structure. One comes up immediately: chlorophyll. Exact match. I throw the result into a chat room. Is there a plant gene in the Z chromosome? How is that possible?

A couple of people respond: others have noticed that too, but nobody knows what to make of it yet.

I go back to the model of the cells produced by the Z chromosome. Chlorophyll. What in burning Io? I zoom out and look at the cells themselves, the way they fit together. Am I really seeing this? A chloroplast. This is definitely a plant gene, not a human gene. How did it get in?

I see it all at once: it was there to begin with. It got in the same way a virus transmittable to humans got into the *Euclid*'s central network.

Guillermo.

Eleven

I look over the various genes being expressed, and one by one I begin to recognize them as either genes from plants or genes that were probably designed by Guillermo himself. The pieces fall into place. Parts of the story are missing still, but it all makes sense. He was redesigning the human body for survival on Helena.

I say it aloud. "Survival!"

Pam looks at me, confused.

"I have to go to the hospital deck," I say. I add a helmet to my skinsuit and dash out the door, run down the corridor to the maglev, and jump in. If I'm right, Haruko and the others have a way to survive until we can find a cure. I call the hospital deck and tell them I need to create a customized environment in a room as close to Haruko's as they can get one. I try to think of what to say on the network to let people know what I'm doing, but everything I can imagine saying sounds absurd.

The maglev stops on the hospital deck, and I get directions from the containment-suited receptionist to the room I'm about to prepare. When I reach the room, I connect the room's atmospheric controller to the satellite uplink from Helena, feeding in the data about Helena's atmospheric composition, average humidity and temperature, everything yet known. Everything known two hundred years ago. And perhaps most important, perhaps what will make the biggest difference: sunlight.

A warning flashes on the door now: Atmosphere unsafe. Risk of CO_2 poisoning. Exactly what I'm looking for. But how to explain to Haruko's doctors? What to say? No time to mull it over. I follow the corridor until I get to her room. The doctors have all three patients in adjoining rooms, and men and women in specialized containment suits that allow for detail work run back and forth from room to room. No one notices me. Finally, I knock on the window. A doctor sees, grabs an assistant, and points at me. The helper comes out.

"This is a medical emergency. What's the matter?"

"The virus is genetically engineered. The Z chromosome is too." The guy looks confused, and I don't blame him. I say, "Your patients aren't human anymore. They're designed for the atmosphere on Helena."

"What?"

"Their skin is turning into chloroplasts to absorb sunlight! The medicating suits you've put them in are what's causing their conditions to worsen—without sunlight, the chloroplasts are dying. I made an environment down the hall that they should be able to survive in."

"You can't be serious."

"Please, I promise this is true."

"Give me data."

No time. No time. I close my eyes in anger, then open them. "Fine. We'll play it your way."

I sit down in a chair in the hall outside the room, open my marble into a network portal, and type up a quick summary of my hypothesis, pointing to the chloroplasts in particular, how efficiently they're stacked into multiple layers, and also to the reflective layer underneath and the micro-ridges in the skin, all the best biological tricks to absorb the most possible sunlight. I list all of the cells produced by the Z chromosome that clearly match cells from other organisms. My hypothesis is that the modified skin absorbs light through the chloroplasts and CO_2 and water from the bloodstream, breaking and forming bonds to produce glucose and free oxygen, which re-enter the bloodstream and return to the lungs, effectively running a second, reverse version of the body's metabolism. All of this needs experimental verification, but how are we to do that but by putting a patient into the proper environment and seeing what happens? The most important thing is sunlight and the removal of the medicating bodysuits that ironically make everything worse by interrupting the transformation. If only the process can be allowed to complete, the skin should regrow its proteins and regain its strength and elasticity. The fragility should be temporary.

I put the summary on the network and flag it as a possible method of surviving the condition. That should get people's attention.

I wait for responses to come in. At first, none do, as if no one who reads this knows what to make of it. It's certainly a lot to take in, but every piece fits. Finally, a comment from Pam. "Can we get another bioengineer's opinion ASAP?"

Nothing. I wait. I close my eyes. Am I wrong? No one knows where the Z chromosome came from, but Guillermo must have somehow seeded it into the population. It just needed the virus to come along and activate it. It makes sense to me. Does it make sense to anyone else? Am I missing something?

I open my eyes. A bioengineer, one whose name I recognize from Path School, comments, "Hypothesis is worth testing. But we need to do so on a smaller or partial scale before risking the life of a patient. Perhaps isolating a limb and observing the body's response."

A second well-known bioengineer concurs with the previous comment. "Worth a shot. The more I look at these skin cells this way, the more the design becomes apparent, even elegant."

That's enough. No one else has suggested a possible survival strategy that's been recommended this strongly. Through the window I see two people go to a matter assembler. They talk back and forth, words I can't hear, and after a minute they stand back. In the assembler appears a transparent sleeve with several microscope attachments and two ports for air flow. They take it to Haruko, remove the current skinsuit her right arm wears, clean the fragile skin on her arm, and place the clear sleeve over it. They attach air tubes that run back to the matter assembler, which they must have set to start producing Helena's atmosphere. That part shouldn't be necessary—the sunlight and removal of skin meds should be enough—but they're testing it holistically first and then isolating the components one at a time later. They set up sun lamps and shine them on her.

Inside the tube, her arm looks dead. The dull color makes me think of gangrene. I remind myself it's the chlorophyll. The more humid air, the sunlight, all of it should start helping soon. I collapse my network portal back into a marble, and curl up in the chair, holding my knees against my chest. I've done all I can for Haruko. Now I have to wait and see.

#

The silence in the corridor numbs my ears. The doctors go about their hurrying, occasionally taking a look through the microscope to see what's happening on Haruko's skin. I can only glance into the room, cannot watch for long periods because of the visible lack of progress. I cannot leave. I cannot look at the network. Only the bare, white ceiling, the empty walls, the slick floor, only these can my vision tolerate from behind the helmet of my suit, whose faceplate rests against my knees.

I close my eyes and see Rio's silhouette floating in front of the orange and blue crescent of Helena's evening atmosphere. I remember the feeling of absolute stillness that comes when I manage to stop drifting in zero gravity. The slight sensation of inertia in my sleep as I felt our home, our *Euclid*, turn.

When I open my eyes, a crowd of doctors blocks Haruko from view. I watch their backs shifting, switching places, and between them I catch a glimpse of green. Not the dull green that Haruko's arm showed before, but a bright, saturated green, vibrant, alive. I uncurl my body, feeling how tight and tense every muscle has become. I get to my feet, stretching the backs of my legs and arching my back before I settle into standing and watching. The doctors change the connections on the apparatus of equipment Haruko lies plugged into, modifying this, removing that, and over the next few minutes she begins to resemble a regular hospital patient, not so many tubes and machines obscuring her body. They expose as much of her skin as possible to the sunlight. It's working.

Finally, a pair of doctors walks quickly to a different room, and through the window I see Haruko's face. She still lies resting in a weak stillness, but her eyes sit open, at last, after a stretch of time that has felt too long to quantify. She watches one of the people at her bedside, then notices me. Our eyes meet. I smile, nearly in tears, and wave at her. She can't move, can't yet wave back, but her eyes stay fixed.

All of the tension and fear in my body deflates, and I can no longer stand. I back up from the window, sit down, and feel in my stomach how long it's been since I've eaten. Can we eat during quarantine? I don't remember the protocol. I can't even think about anything. My head feels light. I should eat.

I stand and fumble my way to the nearest waiting room, ask whoever sits at the service desk about food, and follow his instructions about returning to the room I was in when quarantine started, and using one of the assemblers there. I walk to the nearest maglev stop and wait. Everywhere, the hallways and rooms are still quiet. Inside my helmet, I hear only my breathing. When the maglev comes, I get in and I close my eyes as it propels through the tube. I get off and see no one at the station, see no one in the corridors, and when I get to Pam's lab, she sits exactly where I left her. Have I been gone for hours, or minutes?

She looks up when I walk in.

"Sit down," she says. "You look spent."

I fiddle with the buttons on my skinsuit until my helmet goes away.

"What did I miss?" I say. "I haven't been on the network since my post."

"Sit first."

I comply.

"A lot's come in, actually," Pam says. "The workings of the Z chromosome have been unfolding bit by bit. It looks like people my age may not have anything to worry about. Just like the X and Y sex chromosomes, it has an age range where the secondary characteristics get expressed, and that age range is the one you see in the patients. Young adulthood. It's good news, because likely only a quarter of the ship is at immediate risk instead of two-thirds. But that quarter still has a second puberty coming that we need to deal with. On the plus side, it seems like sunlight, an extra daily liter of water, and a few days of bed rest when the skin is fragile might do the trick. Occasional CO_2 to keep the extra hydrogen ions at bay."

I take it in. My stomach churns and I stand up, go to the assembler, and get a nutrition bar. "Anything about how the chromosome got into the population?"

"That's taking a back seat, but some people are looking into it. It started appearing in the gene pool around a hundred seventy-five years ago. Over a ten-year period, around forty children were born with it, all over the ship. That's common knowledge. What people are looking at now is whose children were they, both biologically and culturally, and who was working at the reproduction clinics at the time. No answers thus far."

I chew the dry, doughy nutrition supplement and wonder.

"Somebody has the answers who's not speaking up," I say.

"That's possible. But it's also true that everyone who was alive then has passed. The oldest person on the ship is only a hundred nineteen, I think."

"Old enough," I say. "Sorry, I need to go again."

Pam holds out a hand. "Stop. Finish your food. You've had enough heroics."

It's true that I may as well finish eating. "This isn't about heroics," I say. "It's about justice. Seeding the population with an extra chromosome without their consent is a crime against dignity."

"We don't know who did it."

"I do. Or I know who designed it."

"How?"

I swallow the last of the food and brush the crumbs from my hands. "He was my brother." I stand up. "Do I still need a helmet?"

"Not at this point."

"Good. I'm sick of being insulated from everything."

I walk out into the corridor, and pull up a network portal on my wrist, scroll until I find Ramakrishnan. His location's set on private, but I know where to look.

#

He floats in the center of the dome, suspended between the two pulls of gravity, so burning perfect at this child's game, so full of secrets and compassionate smiles, and ignoring protocol: no quarantine suit.

"You have answers," I shout up at him from the floor, not bothering to try to jump up, not playing his game. He rotates ever so slowly, drifting in the air.

"It's time to stop keeping secrets," I say. "People have a right to know what's happening to them. The Law of Dignity demands that much, at least."

He turns. He breathes. I can't see his face.

I bend my knees deep and push off, sailing up, past him, and landing on the inside of the dome. I look up. His face is serene, eyes closed, perfectly content.

"You want me to play your game?" I say. "How's this?"

I take out my marble and set it on free form. I stretch it into a globe, smush the globe against the glass until it flattens into a disc. I touch the center of the disc and pull it into a cable, jump with it, stretching it out until I begin to slow, nearing Ramakrishnan, and then I turn off the free form setting. It goes rigid, and I cling to the top of what's now a pole, using one hand to transform the top of it into a network portal.

"Here you go," I say. "Emergency Network Broadcast. Ready to roll?"

He opens his eyes, surveys the scene. "Speaking at length," he says, "will push me away from your screen." Already his equilibrium is broken and he drifts toward the exit.

"Then fall," I say. I drop back to the dome, collapse the disc and pole, and jump, carrying the network portal with me. I pass him, land on the floor before he does, and stand the screen right next to where he falls.

"If you don't tell the colony about Guillermo, and what all of this burning chaos is really about, I will. But I happen to think you can tell the story with fewer holes. You wanted your future where humanity is remade for Helena. Now it's here. But nobody knows what to do with it. Care to tell them?"

His thin, wrinkled skin shines in the light from Helena above us. He looks at me.

"The chaos you see now is quiet. Do you expect it to stay so?"

"I don't care whether you incite this colony into a schism that tears it apart," I say. "It was never one people or one culture to begin with. If this causes people to decide what they really want, that's their right. What I want is the truth. And you have it."

"A small part of it."

"Doesn't make it any less crucial. Speak."

"I leave you with the consequences."

"I can live with that." I push the on-air button.

Twelve

To the colony *Euclid*, I say good afternoon, and I wish you all grace and dignity. You know who I am, or you will soon. One thing you might not know is that you have in your colony a person of dogged will, and you have her to thank for this broadcast.

In my youth I became aware of many events now nearly lost to history because the people involved gave of themselves and their families to make sure the events would stay secret. The era I refer to took place just after the Midflight referendums, which many in the colony feel violated the rights of a large group of people, denying them a true choice by ensuring the dominance of a larger group. Many of them sought to return to Earth. They were denied that. Others among them believed that terraforming Helena, no matter how insignificant its ecosystem might be, amounted to global genocide and to a rebirth of the conquering ideals that ravaged Earth's population before the Second Enlightenment. They believed that if this colony was ever to settle on Helena, it must not be through changing this planet to fit humanity but through the reverse.

They found success in a bioengineer named Guillermo Santiago. His legacy has been erased from the data of the network and instead inhabits the network's physical body, and now your own. He designed the humanity that you've seen begin to emerge in the recent past, and he gave his life to ensure his research would come to fruition. He was not interested in the dignity of his contemporaries as much as he was in the dignity of their descendants. Many like-minded colonists aided in the completion of his life's work, the Z chromosome, seeding it into the population over the course of a decade. I know all of their names, and met some of them in my youth, but all of them have since passed, and I would rather the colony saddle all of their guilt on me than rewrite history to call them criminals. They were not. Their goal, unlike those who hindered their dignity at Midflight, was to give the colony of today a true choice. They have succeeded.

The Z chromosome many of us now carry allows for the possibility of a colony set free of such limitations of space and air as we find both on this ship and on the insignificant bubble colonies near Earth. The new body this chromosome creates gives humanity the chance to inhabit a new world without remaking it in our own image. It gives the people a chance to be set free of the limits of being a single colony, and the chance to form a plurality, to separate into groups as we see fit. While the tenacious young woman who pushed me to speak today may feel that this chromosome limits our freedom, I say that it expands it a hundredfold, both in the present and in the future, when we will not shy from remaking ourselves to shape our own destiny.

Guillermo Santiago and his friends believed in freedom, and lest you think they've left you with not a choice but a command, I tell you that they also believed in human ingenuity. They believed that if you were to reject this choice, to prefer constraint over freedom, that you would find a way to reverse the process. And I have no doubt that given time, a way to remove the chromosome or send it back to its recesses will be found. After all, a simple virus never proved too big a problem for humanity to overcome.

Because I too believe in your freedom, I give you these details: the Z chromosome was designed to have its genes remain recessive and only be expressed when the virus you now struggle with set it loose. This virus was the second piece of Guillermo's magnum opus. He saw DNA being used for storage in the *Euclid*'s network, and saw endless possibilities in the hybrid of biological and electronic components. He programmed the original virus as purely electronic, a way to erase all traces of himself and his research from the historical record, to ensure their secrecy until the correct time. That virus then lay dormant for over a hundred years, destroying anything put into the network that contained his name, his picture, anything that would remind people he had existed.

But knowing the projected date of arrival at Helena, he gave the virus a set of instructions not to be performed until a month or so ahead of that date. Those instructions contained all of the information necessary to assemble a second, biological virus using one of the ship's matter assemblers. And when the date came, the assembler assembled. The organic virus soon ran rampant beside its electronic parent. And now, today, we see its true effects for the first time, in the person of our beautiful Artist Laureate Haruko Kanno, who at this moment is being transferred to a room where the atmospheric conditions of Helena have been recreated. There, the splendor of this new humanity will begin. And with the rest of you, it will continue.

You have only to choose whether you wish to be a part of it.

Do so with grace and dignity.

Thirteen

It's done. I collapse the network portal and put the marble in my pocket. Ramakrishnan looks at me thoughtfully, the sheer oldness of his bald head and white beard no longer casting me into some deep respect. I see him not as a mystery, or even a sage, but a man carrying the relics of an earlier era, who has finally opened the urn to let everyone gaze on the ashes. Anyone can do the things he does, accumulate whatever wisdom he has, if only they live long enough to practice as he has done. I owe him no reverence but that deserved by all people.

I say to him, "Thank you. Goodbye," then turn and walk for the exit.

"Grace and dignity," he says, following whatever his own code may be, a code I no longer feel curious to know. The doors shut behind me.

I walk toward the maglev station, and stop in the corridor when the question of destination tumbles in. I have just done more for the colony, in one day, than I may do in the remainder my life. To whom do I owe something now?

My mother.

The corridor is quiet. Many who were engrossed in emergency measures during the broadcast have not yet seen it, but most of the ship likely has. My parents, for certain, were watching. Whether this will lead to another schism, as in Midflight, to factional fighting, I don't know. The corridor is quiet. I must find my parents.

#

Mom and Dad, I discover while riding the maglev, are home. They are not supposed to be, but they are. When I reach our home, I want to hesitate, but instead force my legs to keep walking until the doors open and I stand in the living room.

My parents stand from their seats at the table. No one speaks.

My father's face tenses expectantly, eyebrows raised, a look of fatigue I've never seen him wear. My mother's face, too, bears exhaustion, expectation, and under it, in her watering eyes, anguish.

The words wait for me to say them. My mother waits.

I'm done with this. No more today can I handle another unmasking, another turning of the *Euclid* in its endless fall toward Helena. I declared a lack of dignity in another person, and I must correct it.

"I'm sorry," I say to my mother, and before I'm finished I am her daughter again. "I'm sorry, Mom."

She presses her lips together and nods. I bury myself in her arms.

#

When we've all calmed down and sat at the table, I hold a glass of water in my lap and notice they both were on the network before I walked in. I ask them, "Why are you home? Did anything happen after the broadcast?"

"The network got very quiet," my father says. "The crowdhack reorganized a little. Your solution is working, so now they're focusing only on reversing the virus's effects. A lot of them still haven't seen the broadcast and are just working with the information supplied by those who have. But that's work for specialists. Most everyone else, I think, has decided to take a break now that the immediate danger of the virus has a remedy. Which I'm very proud of you for suggesting."

I have no emotional energy left to argue about whether he could have suggested it first. I can only say, "Tell me how much you knew. Before today."

My father looks at my mother, and she at him, but so briefly I can't tell what's exchanged in their expressions. More than anything, they both look as spent as I feel.

"Very little," my father says. He clasps his hands in his lap. "We heard the story of Guillermo only as a legend, a myth even. People who'd heard the story passed down said he was murdered because he had succeeded in redesigning humanity, and his research was destroyed by his enemies. But the version told today puts the facts quite differently."

"It was illegal," my mother says. "To tell you, I mean. Because it was opinion. It would have constituted a political indoctrination. If we'd had facts, actual records, those we could have shared."

"That's what I found," I say. "In the archives. Outside the network."

My mother and I stare into each other's faces. "Why did you pick me? What did you hope I'd become?"

"We were asked," my mother says. "Your biological parents wanted their second child to be raised by people who knew the truth about Midflight. They couldn't ensure that, obviously, but they made it known to their friends, their fellow activists in the circle of people who were preserving that knowledge. So along with the story of Guillermo, and the accounts of people who lived through Midflight, their will, as it were, was passed along, too. When the date they specified came, and your mother's egg was fertilized and active in the system, the Children of Midflight asked one of the eligible couples to specifically request your embryo, to fulfill your biological parents' wishes. They didn't want to indoctrinate you, but they wanted to give you the option of joining the cause at its most crucial moment. Which we did."

"And you wanted me to complete Guillermo's work. By pushing me into biotech."

"I wanted to give you the option. The knowledge." She looks at the floor and scrapes her thumbnails together. "I was wrong to push you."

"She's not alone," my father says. "I was wrong to be complicit with her doing so. And knowing the facts, I think Guillermo was wrong, too. The Z chromosome is a masterpiece of genetic modification. But seeding the population was illegal, to say the least. But the people who engineered the Midflight referendums also were wrong. No one is innocent on this ship. We've all either oppressed each other directly or benefited from the oppression of someone else. The test of our character, of our ship's morality, is what we do now that this . . . this situation is upon us. A lot of people with strong opinions are going to speak up, publicly, in the coming days. And that's good. But the fewer voices get raised, the more the mass of humanity leans toward oppression. Because we're all connected to the crimes of the past, we're equal. We need to not lose sight of that."

It sounds like a speech during a lawmaking session. I say to him, "Are you planning to say that publicly?"

He looks at me. "Yes. And whatever your opinion is on this, I advise you to word it carefully and then share it yourself. You have as much right to shape the future of this colony as does anyone else. But unlike everyone else, except maybe Ramakrishnan, you have the weight of the past behind your words. You're as much a link to Midflight as he is."

"I don't know what my opinion is. All I know is Haruko nearly died. A lot of people might have."

"It was negligent," my father agrees. "And many will accuse Ramakrishnan of being the bearer of that negligence. Perhaps justly. Others may be more forgiving. And in the midst of that disagreement, people will look for leaders. Or become them."

Will the next few days bring the debate over what type of colony we should be out of its long simmer and into a boil?

The Law of Dignity demands we not destroy complex, self-aware organisms.

I stand up. Yet one more thing I need to do today. "I need to finish a lab report."

I go into my room and open a network portal. The crowdhack works on curing the virus, and I suspect they'll get there in the next few days. Another teenager came to the hospital deck in the last few minutes, and is going into the Helena environment with the others. The ship still bristles with emergencies.

I open my lab report, scroll to the conclusion, and add a few simple, direct sentences. Nothing inflammatory, hyperbolic, or unfounded. "Synaptic activity, cognition, and self-awareness are all possibilities that cannot yet be ruled out." And that's enough. It's as uncertain as anything else on the network, but the data are what they are. I send it to Pam to look over, though I doubt she'll take the time to do so now. Probably it won't get published online today. But by the time people start pontificating about the virtues of human modification, the evidence will be there that maybe we don't have the right to intrude on this ecosystem, modified or not. Maybe Rio's discovery is the best we can hope for. A bubble colony.

This is the last I can muster today. I expand my furniture marble into a bed, and climb into it. Let society go on without me for a few hours.

#

Somewhere in the long stretch of sleep, I dream I am the *Euclid* herself. Not where I am now, but where I was two hundred and fifty years ago, just before Midflight. Far away from anything and everything, Earth and Io over a hundred fifty years behind, Helena too far to even much consider. So isolated in the emptiness of space that to be on this ship is to notice, from day to day, the infinity of light years, celebrating the passage of each such milestone, marveling at how the distance between yourself and the place your species was born only grows larger, stretches beyond measure. At the peak of my speed, colonists can look out the windows and watch the nearest stars pass each other in parallax. Any nebula, asteroid, comet, planetoid we pass is an event that lasts mere seconds, and years pass between each occurrence.

The colonists busy themselves with their arts and sciences, with caring for one another and for me, the ship. There is nothing else to do. They are generations of stewards, carrying forward the dreams of their great-grandparents, passing those dreams to their great-grandchildren like a torch kept burning for centuries. They paint broad canvasses with imagined landscapes, unable to know what Earth truly was, unable to know what Helena will be. A tribe in the emptiest wilderness sustaining itself, every member treated like family, some succumbing to despair, others to the lust for what little power can be had.

But still I, the *Euclid*, keep flying. Still they survive, sort out what differences they can, grow old, pass away, and keep the flame burning. Never is their ship neglected or forgotten. Young Operations crew replace parts one by one the way a body replaces its cells, and they treat their home with the care of a gardener ensuring her plants have dark soil in which to take root.

Yearly a team of Ops veterans wears pressure suits and climbs up ladders and through airlocks to inspect every inch of the outer hull, each of them stopping, now or then, to look out into the looming black, the impossible extension of size and openness that reaches beyond the event horizon of sight. Those quintessential members of the Midflight generation then turn back toward the precious hull of their colony, and thousands of feet from the nearest airlock or window or dome feel like infants longing to return to the womb. Some succumb, bend to their knees on the hull, and are helped back inside. Others keep on, inspecting the skin of their mother inch by inch, flagging each potential flaw, pushing through their homesickness to continue caring for their ship until they themselves become mothers, and I, the *Euclid*, become their child.

Fourteen

Late in the evening, when I wake, the dream's imagery blurs, but a feeling it stirred lingers deep in my chest. A feeling like the otherworldly climax to Haruko's symphony. Like being homeless, being not of Earth, not of Helena, aliens even to ourselves.

The thought strikes me that I was going to see Haruko tonight, with Rio. So many things have changed, but is it still possible? My stomach constricts and twists with hunger. I've eaten nothing but nutrition bars for the past several meals. Maybe I'll take a few minutes, at least, to have a real dinner before I go. I message Rio while fixing my hair: "Want to see if we can still see Haruko tonight? I'm hoping she'll be well enough for a real visit."

I finish pulling myself together, refreshed from sleep but feeling my brain struggling to get back up to speed, as it always does when I sleep in the afternoon. I come out of my bedroom into the living room, and my straggling mind gives up on pulling itself together when I see Rio standing and talking to my father. They turn and nod at me.

"Edwyn, have you met Rio?" my father says.

I stand frozen in place by how unprepared I am to find khen here. Do I look pulled together enough? "Yeah, I have. Is everything all right?"

"We were discussing the possibility of a bubble colony on Helena," Rio says. "I'm preparing a few remarks to present alongside my lab's findings."

My thoughts still swirl, clouded by the dream. "Present where? I'm sorry, I needed to get some sleep."

"Understandable," Rio says. "A lot of people are asking about you on the network."

Adrenaline kicks in, and I give my head a shake and decide to be completely awake now. "OK, you all need to fill me in. What happened in the last few hours?"

"They found the assemblers responsible for manufacturing the virus, and stopped them," my father says. "They've got a possible lead on a cure, too: a modified version of the virus itself that reverses the changes at the DNA level. It may have to be customized for each person, but that's not a hurdle when we have everyone's gene sequences on file. Another few days, a week at the most, and all this will be figured out."

"Except people deciding if they want the cure," I say. Images come to me of what may happen soon, crowds of suddenly green-skinned people sitting and talking, comforting each other in Helena-like rooms, their genomes modified without their consent. Many of them horrified, others confused, a few perhaps even excited now that the worst has passed. All of them forced to choose what shape their humanity will take.

"Public voicing of responses to the crisis is encouraged," Rio says. "All research except that on the virus has been declared optional for tomorrow. It's kind of a holiday for people to collect themselves. The day after, public statements from colonists are being scheduled."

"Is that where Mom is?" I say. "Helping decide all that?"

My father smiles. "Yes. And it won't be a holiday for everyone. I'll be leading group counseling sessions all day long. A lot of people are going to need someone to listen."

"What about you? Don't you get to . . . collect yourself?"

"It's part of my job to be collected all the time," he says. "Most of these scenarios we face I've thought about before. It's only the specific circumstances that are disconcerting. Knowing your mother has many advantages. We've talked about the pros and cons of every type of human modification and colonization you can think of. These aren't new issues. They've just become more pressing."

Rio says, "I came to ask his . . . reading of the ship's pulse, so to speak."

Still uncertain how to act in the presence of both my father and Rio, I go to the assembler and scroll through the meals, looking for something I can savor quickly, if that's not an oxymoron. "So what's your reading?" I say. "How's the ship doing?"

My father opens a cushy chair from his marble and sits in it. "The strongest single current I've seen in the ship's subconscious for years now is a kind of longing. The blue sky projected above the corridors reminds people of skies they've never seen in person. Films of Earth make them wonder what real outdoor air smells like. The history of this ship and what happened above Io tells them that life on *any* ship simply isn't good enough.

"We have parks and ponds and even a mock mountain on this colony, and people go there, and in their subconscious it reminds them of the real Earth, but Earth, for all of us, exists as little more than a genetic memory, a place our bodies adapted themselves to that's now so far distant we have only small pieces of it. Beneath our everyday activities, our research, lawmaking, maintaining the ship, maintaining each other, there flows this undercurrent, this wishing for something we can't define. Even I can't. The best I can do is go into one of those simulators like you use for your research, set it on some Earth environment, and sit there until I convince myself that if I got up and walked, I could keep going, that I wouldn't eventually hit a wall, a hull, the vacuum of space."

He takes a long breath, looking at nothing. "I've wondered at times if I'm merely projecting, if it's only me who feels this way, but the sessions I give tell me otherwise. Humans, on some level, are psychologically inseparable from the environment that formed us. We can approximate it, but never duplicate it. We can never make another Earth."

I've been eating while listening to him, and looking at my pasta and broccoli with a sense of separation. Earth gave us the plants that made this meal, but its matter came from the assembler. If I select the same meal tomorrow, it will have the same arrangement of pasta, the same florets of broccoli, same sprinkling of garlic and oil, all the way down to the atom.

"Then wouldn't a bubble colony feel just the same as a ship?" I say. "Wouldn't it still feel closed?"

"To many, perhaps," Rio answers, though I asked my father. "But if I may, I think a large part of the collective unconscious claustrophobia to which your father refers comes from the tangibility of this colony's boundaries. Given a large enough open space, and given boundaries that are not easily accessible, the impression of limitation would greatly diminish."

Khe sits down across the table from me and makes broad gestures with khes hands. "Imagine a colony that has a large enough bubble that it's hard to even reach the end. Surrounding not just an island, but a mile of the sea all around it, the rock underneath, the sky above. You would have to get into a boat and sail before you found the walls."

I twist my fork, wrapping the long strips of pasta around it. "I think people like my mother, people like Ramakrishnan, still wouldn't be satisfied. They'd need to set foot on the other side of the bubble. Earth was only big enough because we were on the outside of the sphere instead of the inside. And then, even Earth wasn't enough, was it?"

I laugh, but it's humorless. "People had to see what was out in space. It may not even be Earth itself that people long for, but for the absence of limits. Evolution is the history of competition and cooperation, of environmental forces killing some, sparing others. If people are going to be happy, we need, I don't know, to feel like there's nothing holding us back. Like we really have freedom." I think back to what Ramakrishnan said, that first time I saw him at the Children of Midflight's gathering. "I don't think we'll be satisfied until we can breathe and live even inside a stellar fusion reaction."

Rio listens to me, never looking away. Then khe smiles. "And who's to say we can't? We found a way to survive for over four centuries in space. I think we can go quite a bit further given enough time. You seem to equate the absence of physical limits with freedom, but maybe it's not the physical limits that are important."

"What other kinds of limits are there?" I say.

"You mentioned cooperation. I would have, too. When you participated in the crowdhack, at the beginning, what did you feel?"

"Mostly stress, adrenaline."

"What else?"

I think about it. There was a kind of power in having so much data to draw from, a power in being connected to so many others who held the same objective. "I'm not sure. A sense of possibility, maybe. Or purpose. Is that what you're getting at?"

"Here's what I felt," Rio says, and before khe even speaks, at those words alone, that serious yet enthusiastic candor, I fall for khen all over again. "I felt the expansion of self. It's easy to forget that everything we're talking about, all this claustrophobia, because it's psychological, is inside us. So the only solution we need is a psychological one. I contributed what little I knew of biology to the mix today, but what was more important was what I knew about everything else. My ability to look at the data with eyes that were different from everyone else's. That's what makes crowdhacks work: the cross-pollination of knowledge. In those minutes, those hours, even now, all of those working together are sensing not their own limitations but how much less limited, how much more expansive, is a collective mind, a community working in concert.

"The Second Enlightenment, the collaborative economy, made extraterrestrial colonies simple, and also made the *Euclid* possible. What's most achievable now is not the sense of physical freedom or power, but collective freedom, collective power. We don't need to transcend physical boundaries. We need to transcend the limited sense of self we impose on our consciousness. Feeling that we're a functional part of something bigger than ourselves makes physical limits less significant. We'll feel that we are bigger than the space we inhabit."

In the silence that follows, I feel both awed by and infatuated. People are going to listen to my public opinion when people like Rio have much wiser things to say? The *Euclid* I grew up in is not the *Euclid* I inhabit now. I'm still getting to know her. How am I to presume to change something I still don't understand?

Rio looks at the table now, muttering to khenself. "It's the colony in concert."

All at once, I get an idea. Complex yet fully formed: a pure, complete image.

"Haruko," I say. "We should go see Haruko."

Rio looks at me. "You think we can?"

"I designed the burning Helena room she's in." I say. "If no one else, they'll let me in."

"We'll need suits," Rio says.

"Whatever. Physical boundaries don't need to be significant, right?"

Khe smiles. "I like the way you think."

Nothing anyone can ever say will mean more to me than that. "Let's go."

We stand up, and I kiss my father on the cheek as we pass him. "I'll be back," I say.

"Remember the people at the hospital are still having a rough day," he says.

"Not much chance I'll forget that."

#

In the maglev pod, Rio and I talk back and forth about the rough specs for the bubble colony khe intends to present, about ways to keep its boundaries natural, invisible, and ways to make its cities about connection, community, collective strength. We bounce ideas off each other without judgment, just playing with possibility.

When we get out on the hospital deck, I jump out of the maglev pod.

"Io, I can't wait to hug her." I say.

Rio follows but says nothing. Has khe lost that level of familiarity with her?

We follow the corridors toward the Helena room. I open my marble into a network portal and download a smaller helmet for my quarantine suit, one that won't get in the way. I interface the marble with my clothes and stop for just a breath until the new suit covers me. Rio puts on a suit of khes own. Oddly, the halls seem empty. Is everyone buried in the crisis still? Several of the doors we pass flash the same environmental warning that the Helena room did. Preparation for a crowd of mutating young humans if the cure isn't ready in time. Those affected don't need the CO_2 to breathe, but the doctors have decided to give their patients' new, second metabolism a chance to function fully.

We get to Haruko's room, and have to step close to the door to let an airlock seal itself around us before the door will open. When it does, I see an open space streaming with bright sunlight, the ceiling and upper walls of the room not literally removed but appearing so, a pale blue sky and blinding sun making the room feel exposed to the elements. Haruko sits up in her bed in a two-piece leotard, free of all her machines and equipment, shining green arms and legs and torso taking in the sun. Only a hand-sized device on her chest monitors her vitals closely. A doctor in a quarantine suit of his own sees us and leaves her side to come over.

"We're not allowing visits until the emergency is resolved."

"Two minutes, I promise," I say. "Please. I'm sure she'll be better for it."

Haruko is already out of bed and walking over to us herself. The doctor turns as if to protest, but she hurries over to me and we hug tight. Quickly I let her go. "Is your skin okay for that?"

"It's fine," she says. "It's strong now." Her face looks different with the reflective green so thick and bright. "You are brilliant," she says.

I can't help smiling, though I'm not yet comfortable with the praise. Maybe this is how she felt when everyone was congratulating her on her symphony. Like she had worked hard, sure, but didn't everyone?

She turns to Rio. "Come here," she says, and gives khen a quick hug, too, though khe lets go quickly.

"You look much healthier," khe says.

"I feel fantastic compared to this morning," she says. "I still haven't been able to catch up on everything that's happened. I saw the broadcast though."

"I keep waiting for a riot," I say. "A lot of people have to be angry about this, but they must be channeling it somewhere."

"There are a number of arguments calling for a referendum," Rio says. "To try Ramakrishnan for crimes against dignity. Not all of them worded kindly."

"I believe it," Haruko says. "Oh, but there's news. It isn't much, but the doctors have a theory as to why I didn't have any virus cells in me when this showed up," she holds up her green hand and turns it around, "they think the virus dies off after its rewrite of the DNA is complete. Basically, since I was the first infected, I got the most 'accurate' form of the virus, before it had a chance to evolve and vary slightly from its program. It started out pretty contained, but once it spread exponentially about two days ago, the two new patients were exposed to a much higher number of virus cells than I was, many of which survived longer than they were designed to. If the virus hadn't started to evolve on its own, it would have covered its tracks more quickly."

I shake my head. "This Guillermo had to be obsessed."

"It's kind of incredible how much information he put into that original computer virus," Haruko says. "They're trying to decrypt some of those files that have been roaming the network for two hundred years. If you ask me, the day after tomorrow is way too soon to start public comments. But I guess putting it off would just cause a buildup."

"Actually, I came to ask you something important about that," I say. "Can you give me a crash course in conducting?"

She looks at me like I've asked her to stop being green. "I doubt it. I'm research subject number one right now. Well, number two, after the virus itself."

"Can you refer me to someone?"

"I guess so. What does this have to do with public comments?"

"I'm not planning on just making a speech."

The doctor kicks us out shortly thereafter, and Rio and I again leave the hospital together. Khe's only a couple inches taller than me, though for a while now I've imagined khen as maybe a head higher. With the various times I've pushed around people in the past day or so, refusing to relent until they listened to me, how much more difficult should it be to ask a person I like, really like, if khe'd be interested in spending more time with me tonight?

As we enter the maglev stop, I take Rio's hand in mine. Khe squeezes back, ever so slightly, barely perceptible, but doesn't pull away. I look at khes eyes, and say, "Where would you like to go?"

Khe looks back at me. Seconds pass. Has khe ever looked at me this long, just looked?

"I don't know," khe says. "I hadn't planned the day this far."

"Feel like floating?" I say.

Khe doesn't look thrilled at the idea, but doesn't say anything against it, either.

I squeeze khes hand tighter. Like waking from a dream I realize khe looks terrified. I smile at khen. "We don't have to," I say. "I just thought it would be nice. I won't bite."

Khe jokes, with a nervousness that desires a serious answer, "What will you do, then?"

Io, I wish I could kiss khen right there, this honesty and beautiful intelligence and trust all I want in a human being. I face khen and take khes other hand in mind, holding them between us. "I'll drift with you and hold your hands if that's all you want," I say.

And we go. We get a two-seated maglev pod and keep our fingers interlocked. We go to the room khe likes, the one we've been to before, and set it on a program with lots of stars. Galaxies everywhere you turn. And we float together, arms connecting us like a tether at first, then pulling us side by side, holding each other at the waist. Then khe's behind me, khes arms crossed over my abs, khes cheek against my ear, our fingers linked, my back against khes chest. We drift, touch the cushioned wall, and with one hand I hold onto the soft surface and keep us there. I turn my head, and kiss Rio's neck below the ear.

Khe turns, we rub our noses together, then lips, once, then a second kiss, a longer, softer one. I hold khes hand tight as we become fog, fade into nothing but the moment, the delicate tactile senses of each other, the warmth, the trust, the simple intimacy of having our faces touch. We inhabit each meeting of skin, each kiss in its own fleeting universe. One last, lengthening moment before our lips part and Rio turns away, khes cheek to my ear again. I pull khen closer, curl my legs up, and feel khes thighs warm against the backs of mine. We rest against the cushion, and little by little, on a gradual timer, gravity returns to the sphere. My free-floating hair falls softly down. We sink into the cushioned wall that has now become a cushioned floor, and we sink into each other and into sleep.

Fifteen

Darkness shrouds the still room when I wake. Rio is gone. I sit up and scan through my messages. One from Rio: "Sorry to leave so early. Tried to wake you to say bye, but you wouldn't budge. Still a busy day for me, but love to talk to you tonight."

The day for the colonists to collect themselves. Will it bring a tide of public messages tomorrow, or something much worse? All of the ship's chaos lives behind closed doors. I reach to set my skinsuit on shower mode, and the touch of my own hand on my wrist console brings back Rio's arms from last night. I hold myself around the waist and around the shoulder, and remember. Closeness. I shut my eyes, sit still a moment, and inhabit the memory.

Then I let it go for now. I open my marble into a network port, and make a list for the day: prepare an introductory speech—be brief. Find interested singers. Remember the dream of walking on the hull of the *Euclid*. Find that moment, and, be realistic, someone else to conduct it. There's no time today for me to learn what I would need to conduct it myself. Find Hesper and Isaac. Find mom. Keep an eye on the network.

My stomach reminds me it's morning. I can finish the list over breakfast. I pack up the marble, stand up, and make for the door.

The corridor ceiling only faintly shows the light before dawn, a distant gray. All is quiet. The public farms and cafeterias are closed, nonessential Operations crew sent home, as many souls as possible given a break from research, service, and duty. Many of them may share their troubles with my father or another counselor. Others may not venture further than friends or loved ones for advice; still others will have already made up their minds what they and the rest of the ship ought to do. This last group is the most potentially dangerous, yet I count myself among them, ideas and words coming together in my mind for the speech I must give if I am to participate in this moment of history.

I find a food assembler at one of the empty cafeterias, take my breakfast to a table, and write while I eat. I've never seen the ship this silent, the corridors so empty. The hush of pre-dawn Orbit Day carried the energy and anticipation of a new era. Today, what hovers in the purified air may be more akin to fear. Today is a day for quiet chaos. Tomorrow, people make noise.

#

I spend the morning and early afternoon writing and searching through databases for precisely what words and sounds I want to share with the colony, and for people to help me share them. When afternoon comes, I leave the task half-finished, and leave the still empty cafeteria. In the hours I've spent there I've seen no other person. But I have convinced Hesper and Isaac to meet me in one of the parks for lunch. It feels as if an epoch of the ship's history has expired since I've last seen them.

The closer I get to the park, the more I see people coming and going. Still a hush dampens everything, a solemnity like mourning in the way people talk in low tones, aware of disagreements in the air, choosing words with precision. On the grass and under the trees and wading in the lake, families enjoy the most realistic sunshine the ship has to offer, the artifice of the corridors strangely apparent. I find Hesper and Isaac at a picnic table, a mobile food assembler hovering in the grass next to them. They both stand as I approach, and I take Hesper first into my arms, a rare, full embrace from one who doesn't often touch, her softness like the sun.

Then I hug Isaac, his hard, thin arms squeezing me almost to pain.

"It's been days," Isaac says. "Seems like months, doesn't it?"

"A long time, anyway," Hesper says.

They both look at me, and at first I have no words to say to them. "How are you both doing?" I ask at last. Nothing else seems important.

Isaac looks contemplative. "I feel like an asteroid," he says, "floating along through space doing whatever, not a care in the galaxy, and then thrown into the gravity well of a red giant about to go nova, and what in burning Io is going on?"

"I wouldn't go quite that far," Hesper says. She sits back down at the picnic table. "For me it's more like stepping off a gravitied wall onto a gravitied floor. That one moment when you're turning and you can't tell which way is up. Once you've gotten to the second surface, it takes you a moment to get reoriented, and that moment is lasting a long time. And hey, congratulations on finding the very first candidate for complex cognition on an exoplanet." Her smile goes wide. "That's a milestone that's worth remembering, I don't know, a thousand years from now?"

"I haven't even had time to get excited about that," I say. "Who does? Even historical, groundbreaking discoveries feel less urgent than making sure the colony doesn't fall apart."

"We'll find time to go nova over astrobiology soon," Hesper says. "Once all this craziness settles down." She waves at Isaac and me to sit down with her. "Speaking of which, what are you up to today? Are you making a public comment tomorrow?"

"Planning on it."

"You look like you just had a light year of gym lectures," Isaac says. "You okay?"

"Yesterday was pandemonium," I say. "One thing after another after another. I'm expecting tomorrow to be the same."

"What are you going to say?" Hesper says.

"Not too much, if I can help it." I pull out my marble, expand it to a reading pad, and open my draft of the speech. I hand it to her. She reads, nods, reads. "Might need some fine-tuning," she says, "but I really like the gist of it." She hands it to Isaac. "What's the choir going to sing?"

"Still figuring that out," I say. "It needs to fit thematically with what I'm saying, but I'm also trying to express a particular feeling. You ever wake up in the middle of the night and realize just how small this colony really is, and how impossibly large, terrifying, and beautiful the universe is?"

They're both silent. Isaac says, "I do. Actually, I've been feeling that all day. And I think I know what you're looking for. Try one of this guy's compositions. See what you think." He hands me back the pad. There's a new tab open with the profile of a composer and his major works. "Thanks," I say. "This is . . . yeah, this has potential."

"Two heads are better than one," Isaac says.

Hesper turns to me conspiratorially. "You should say that tomorrow. Instead of green skin, we should all give ourselves a second head. Two brains. Think about it."

I laugh. "I think I'll stick closer to the wording I already have." But it's been too long since I've had a laugh, and it lingers inside. Like a door staying open.

#

The rest of the day disappears in the work of revising my speech and sharing it with interested choir members so they fully understand the message informing whatever music we'll sing. I sit at a table outside the park, drawing on the silence of strangers for the energy to keep pushing myself.

I listen to piece after piece by Eric Whitacre, the composer Isaac recommended, nothing feeling quite right. After hours without success, I go back and listen to some of them again, giving them a second chance, and one grabs me. It's not perfect, but I flag it for later use. After re-listening to some others, I come back to it again, read the poetry it sets to music, and decide it's close enough.

I send a message to my father, asking him for the names of the choir members he mentioned a few days ago, those for whom music is a way to make sense of the world, and I ask him if any of them know how to conduct.

While waiting for a response, which he won't send until he has a break between sessions, I send the Whitacre piece to the members who have agreed so far, making sure they're still up for it. By evening, I've recruited just over twenty singers, far less than ideal given that the piece breaks into fourteen simultaneous voice lines at one point, but enough people to carry it. I juggle their various plans for tonight and tomorrow, and schedule a tentative rehearsal time for early tomorrow morning, before my scheduled slot to speak.

I ask the choir members directly if anyone is able and willing to conduct. I read the score for the piece and listen to it over and over, tweaking my speech, and seeing more parallels the longer I study it. It's going to work. It really is. I just need someone to bring the singers, myself included, into the most apt performance. I can't do it alone. I laugh to myself at the truth of that. I read over my speech again and again, changing words, cutting lines to keep it as short as possible and put more focus on the performance.

The lights dim. The day has passed quickly. I send Rio a message asking if khe wants to meet me for dinner. Khe's still working on khes own presentation. I invite khen to the rehearsal tomorrow. Khe can't do it, but promises to watch my broadcast. I suppose it's selfish of me to steal khes time on such a day. I catch myself hoping the ship's crises will quiet down soon, or get resolved quickly, though I know how unrealistic such a hope is likely to be.

Nothing left to do tonight but wait for responses. I walk the corridors home, skipping the maglev because I've been sitting all day. Maybe by the time I get home, someone will have agreed to conduct. The hall ceilings darken to stars. I stop in an empty stretch of corridor and look up at them, putting myself back in that dream, that intensity of needing a secure place, a home, amid the unfathomable emptiness of space.

#

At home I find my mother in the living room, working on her own speech. She gets up from it when I come in. She stands up and we hug briefly.

"You've been busy," she says.

"You too?"

"You know me," she says. All of the moments over the past week when I felt I didn't understand her at all come flooding back. But the wave recedes. After everything that's happened, I now feel like I do know her. Mostly. I'm still unsure what to expect from her speech.

She catches me glancing at it.

"It's long right now," she says. "I spent all day writing it. I'm trying to sift through, prioritize the most important things."

"Need any help?" After I say it I wish I hadn't. I don't know how much I can handle.

"I'm not looking for debate," she says. "I mean, not yet. What I need most is objectivity, a pair of eyes that knows what my views are, and can help me emphasize and clarify them regardless of whether he agrees."

He. Dad. He must still be doing sessions. Seeing her in a place where she can't get his help is rare enough that it's always a surprise, a reminder how much she relies on him to keep herself honest.

"I've already got my speech down," I say. "I can take a break from my argument a while."

She smiles at me, then pulls me close and kisses my hair. "I'm glad your bio-parents waited," she says. She holds me again, more tightly this time. I lose myself in it like a blanket.

She lets go, and squeezes my shoulder before sitting down.

"Here's the outline," she says. "It should make pretty clear what I want to emphasize most."

"Thanks," I say. For a second, I can't take my eyes from her. She is a person, dignified as we all are, and she loves me. She waits for me to say something. "Thank you," I finally say again, and I believe she catches the meaning I intend.

#

Morning comes once again. I've had the music in my head all night, and it's all I remember of my dreams. The voices, the dissonance, the harmony. No one has responded to my requests for a conductor, so I eat a quick breakfast and leave for rehearsal. I'll have to improvise, even if it means finding footage of the original composer conducting the piece and playing that without sound in front of the choir.

Already the corridors are alive with people, an energy so different from yesterday's that I know, yet again, something must have happened during the night. I'm afraid to look, despite how positive the mood of the populace seems, people passing me and smiling, nodding at me as if I've had some hand in whatever took place.

I walk into the choir room we arranged, and everyone stands from their chairs. People my age and twice or three times my age, gathered to help me make a statement I can only hope bears some truth. People I've sung with before and people I've never met.

"Good morning," I say, oddly more nervous about addressing them now than about the speech I'm giving in an hour or so. "I can't tell you all how much it means to me to have your help. I am going to have to ask one more time for a volunteer, or we may find ourselves singing without a live conductor."

The singers laugh, but it's not a cruel one. I sense something amiss.

"I'd like to volunteer," someone says, and I recognize her voice before I turn around and see her behind me, she having hidden just inside the door. Haruko. She's wearing a suit that must be giving her skin mobile sunlight on the inside, skin still green as ever, but she looks as happy and strong as I've ever seen her.

"You told me—" I begin.

"Things change," she says. "The day before yesterday I still felt weak. Today I feel great, and my second metabolism can handle a few hours without CO_2. I don't have to stay in the lab either."

"Why not?"

"They finished the cure. Posted it on the network a couple hours ago."

I turn to the choir. Everyone's smiling, joyous even.

"Well," I say, trying not to let loose all the things I'm feeling, trying not to completely break down. "We'd better practice if we're going to get this right. Haruko, you'll need the music."

"I have it. I've been listening to it ever since you posted it on the conductor request yesterday."

I have to hug her. She lets me.

"And you're sure you'll be okay?"

"I felt worse the day I conducted my own symphony. Still did it then."

I take my place among the sopranos. Haruko takes a moment to breathe and pull herself together, then steps to the front of the choir.

#

We mess up. We fix it. We break the piece into sections and do what Haruko tells us. I have complete, total faith in her instincts and understanding of the piece, and she leads us with a vigor beyond her medical suit. We put all the pieces together, and it's almost perfect, not there yet, but almost. Haruko wants us to do it once more, but I have to stop her.

"It's time," I say. "My spot's coming up in a couple minutes."

Haruko thinks for a moment. Then she says to the choir, "Okay. This time we get it right."

I open a network portal on the wall. I take a last look at my speech, then close the tab, still nervous, but certain that I will say everything I need to.

The choir stands ready behind me. In the broadcast, their crowd of faces in the background will frame mine. There are over fifty channels of comments being broadcast at the moment, but my father believes I will be listened to. I take him at his word.

The screen flashes. I'm on the air.

"Hello," I say. No idea who I'm speaking to, but whoever they are, they are colonists. Humans. People. What else matters? "My name is Edwyn Santiago. I make this comment as a citizen of the *Euclid*, no more or less. The views I share are my own, but I couldn't have come to them without the aid of everyone on this ship. And I don't know what's best for the *Euclid*. But the point I make today is that I don't need to.

"Let me use an example. Around two hundred years ago, a referendum was designed to systematically cast a minority view out of the general discourse. I've seen enough evidence in the historical record to believe this was intentional. Under the guise of democracy, a group of colonists was oppressed. The referendum ensures each individual voice is heard, but what it leaves out is the voice of the colony as a whole.

"But what's the difference? Let me use another example. The dedicated scientists on this ship, which include me but also thousands of others, have been working nonstop to resolve the current crisis. This morning, they found a cure. You found a cure. How did we do it? With a crowdhack. Could we have voted on it? The idea is absurd. It was not a problem to solve by voting. It could only be solved by concerted action. And back at Midflight, we faced an equal problem: a faction of the colony that wanted to go home. But we rewrote the problem as a question: *should* we go home? And we voted on it.

"This was a mistake. It turned what should have been a problem to be collaboratively solved into a competition of who had more people on their side. It's easy to rewrite our current situation into a series of questions. 'Should we colonize Helena?' 'Should we do so as conventional humans?' 'Should we do so as modified humans?' To put such questions to a vote turns them into competitions instead of the collaborations that allowed our forebears to found this colony. Doing so also ignores the best chance we have at resolving these issues as a society, because making them into questions forces us to answer as individuals.

"The mistakes of Midflight must not be repeated: the future of our colony should not be put to a vote. It should be crowdhacked, just as Midflight should have been."

There. I've made my argument. Now for the important part.

"If you've ever had a moment where the walls of the *Euclid* feel thin and fragile, where the universe feels endlessly large and empty, where you feel like we as a people are so isolated from and maybe even forgotten by the place from which we came, then you know that this ship is the only safe home we have.

"I'd like to perform for you today a piece of music that resonates with my experience of that feeling, and that knowledge. It also demonstrates collaboration.

"Eric Whitacre's piece 'Water Night' cannot be performed live without at least fourteen singers. Even Whitacre himself could not have composed it without the poetry of Octavio Paz, whose words he set to music. I would be foolish to attempt performing it on my own.

"Thank you for listening."

I step back from the network portal, and join the choir. I open the sheet music.

Haruko takes my place before us, and raises her hands.

She brings us in on the flat, minor, dissonant chord that begins the piece, a serene meshing of voices that in spite of its conflicting tones carries a placidity and intricacy, the vibrations in my chest and head flowing out into a smooth, suddenly pleasing high as the men's and women's intonations rise in pitch, volume, and speed, then fall, slowing as if to catch breath on a long climb down a mountain:

Night with the eyes of a horse that trembles in the night,

The women's voices fall back, letting the deep, darker sounds of the men give the next half-line an ominous clash, but then they return, the high, smooth female voices reassuring that hope remains. They alternate taking the lead, the men calling and the women responding, neither fully dropping away but carrying a quieter, second layer over one another. In my body the sound hums from my skull down into my abdomen, my voice melding with the others like a ringing drum joining a circle, then fading as the choir again slows and quiets:

night with the eyes of water in the field asleep
is in your eyes, a horse that trembles,
is in your eyes of secret water.

Then it comes, the women breathing in and letting out a sudden, loud, sustained minor chord, the men waiting, then joining, for just a moment the choir shouting as one in a resounding, powerful dissonance that stretches from high to low at once, as if struggling to express what cannot be expressed, the experience of beauty no human can ever fully communicate to another. We try again, slower, quieter, and a third time, fading to the most painful clash, the most jarring combination of sounds in the piece, the women fading first, leaving the deepest male voices to carry the uncomfortable noise:

Eyes of shadow-water,
eyes of well-water,
eyes of dream-water.

How to respond to a division and dissidence so deep that it culminated in oppression, a wound by the hand of the majority that ultimately hurt us all? How to heal from it? The voices fade almost to nothing, and come back hesitantly, first the men, nearly whispering, voices of emptiness. The women return with climbing, loudening, clear, glassy notes, encouraging, and the men again join them. Together, they build in strength and volume, still dissonant, then moving toward more harmonious layers, never quite getting there but in the process arriving at a stirring resonance of anticipation:

Silence and solitude,
two little animals moon-led,
drink in your eyes,
drink in those waters.

A slight pause, a sudden silence in the building sounds, our conductor frozen, and then bursting with movement: the four sections of us erupt in a moment of pure harmony, still somehow dissonant yet breathtaking, the choir splitting into over a dozen different tones sung simultaneously, the dissonance no longer a tension or conflict but a proud, open unfolding of mellifluous layers and musical texture, the energy carrying us forward through an unseen gate, the sopranos, myself among them, releasing from our strong lungs a wave of joyous consonance in the climactic verse:

If you open your eyes,
night opens, doors of musk,
the secret kingdom of the water opens,
flowing from the center of the night.

The last word extends, relaxes, quiets, fades.

In its wake, the final verse, a denouement of solace and rest, opens with a melodic flow that reassures us whatever dissonance, whatever conflict or disagreement remains is real and good and true, our voices rising and falling in waves of volume and echo, retaining the clash we've been fighting against, reveling in the multiplicity of voices and tones, letting the in and out of our vibrating bodies carry us until we quiet once more on the penultimate line:

And if you close your eyes,
a river fills you from within,
flows forward, darkens you:

And on the final line of the song, we release whatever is left, Haruko's arms moving in graceful curves, guiding us over a musical echo that hearkens back to the opening notes but retains none of their ominousness, then runs through the familiar fading and falling until, on the final word, we resolve the chord, vary a few voices up, then down, a final wave, and resolve the chord again, the singers and listeners arriving at last at the musical destination:

night brings its wetness to beaches in your soul.

Haruko's arms fall to her sides. She bows at us. She bows at the camera, then steps aside and raises her arm, directing the audience to us. We bow. No applause is audible, but in the silence, as we lower our heads, I see beyond us the listening families in their rooms, the doctors and scientists working to give the infected a chance to reverse their changes, the bright green modified colonists waiting urgently or marveling at themselves in their Helena rooms, farmers adjusting water and light in hydroponics bays, lonely colonists sitting in empty domes and gazing into open space, the operations crew keeping our one certain home alive and ever in orbit.

I feel, can almost see or touch, the joy and the dignity of everyone in the room, of all those aboard listening or not listening. Everyone. It permeates the air.

Sixteen

On my knees, I dig my fingers into the cool, dark soil of the greenhouse. Sun lamps on the ceiling brighten the white walls, fans pump air and humidity into the chamber, and I dig small holes to plant green seedlings in rows for later harvest. The density of microbes in the soil, the water vapor in the air, the smell of tomato plants on my fingers—everything smells of Earth. I can never be sure what the air on a mountain or by the ocean smelled like, but I'm certain that greenhouses on Earth smelled just like this, that the smell of soil is the smell of home.

Great-grandma brings over a tray of seedlings ready to be planted. Not since I was in early Prime School have I accompanied her in her volunteering, and when I smelled the greenhouse again this morning, I asked myself how I could let so many years pass without breathing in such denseness of life.

I stand, thank her, take the tray, and kneel again. I take the first seedling from the tray and place it in the hole. It will stay small a few weeks, but like the hydroponic-grown plants in other greenhouses on the ship, it will eventually grow so tall as to need a cage to hold it up.

The continent-sized organisms on Helena, one on each of the two largest continents, may engage in thought at such slow intervals that coming to understand what consciousness is to them could take years; to find a method of communication, years more, if ever.

It's a disappointing reality, that major discoveries are bigger than us, that one generation may not be enough to transform data into knowledge.

But still: patience, Pam always reminded me. I smile at that now. I imagine taking weeks or months to think a single thought. Years to have a simple conversation. These organisms, if they can perceive us at all, would see us flitting on invisibly-blurred wings like a flock of hummingbirds, moving at breakneck speed, while they, ever slowly, grow at speeds more akin to those of the cosmos, their lifespan more like that of a planet itself.

Unraveling the knot of their existence, slow-going as the work might be, gives everyone on board something new to look forward to, a destination for future colonists to travel toward, a second leg of our journey. I myself look forward to simply returning to the lab tomorrow, after taking a week away from research and from most things, once I'd given my speech.

In the hours and days that followed it, I listened to broadcasts, watched the faces of hundreds of colonists describe their responses and views on the crisis: farmers, pilots, doctors, librarians, mechanics, geologists, bioengineers, politicians, friends, family. Children, young adults, older colonists, great-grandparents.

The diversity itself gives me comfort, that while numerous voices directly opposed mine, and called for referendums I dislike, their voices mixed with those of many others so that the only concrete, collective thoughts that emerged from the broadcasts were these: we must keep researching the Z chromosome, the planet, its life, and ourselves. Those with a Z must retain the freedom to accept the cure or to live as modified humans. Any process of colonization must follow the Law of Dignity. All this, to the people of the *Euclid,* remains self-evident.

Public debates, many which my mother joined and a small number which I joined myself, were constant, and will continue to be. Some days, after disagreeing in public, my parents and I sat down to dinner, and all three of us still found something to fault in each other's words. Things can get uncomfortable. But I accept this. At the end of the day, I remind myself, we are not making the same mistakes. We are not jumping to decide everything quickly by vote.

I put the last seedling into its hole, tuck the soil in around it, and stand. Great-grandma kneels further down the row, and I watch her. How many years it must have taken for her to shed all the stresses people like me carry. I walk between the lines of seedlings toward the end of the greenhouse to grab another tray, having nothing planned for the day but a late dinner with Rio. I've seen khen only twice this past week, both of us busy with our families or with low-stress activities like this planting, which the ship's counseling committee recommended in the wake of the public broadcasts. The little time Rio and I have we spend talking, or not talking, and khe becomes one more slow process of discovery in my life.

My father was right: there's no hurry anymore. Our colony can debate as long as it needs to. Later generations can unearth deeper insight into Helena and her lifeforms. Rio and I can orbit each other as long as we need, and if we grow as lovers or decide to grow into friends, there's no deadline.

When I finish planting for the day, I stand between the rows, spread my bare arms, and throw back my head as the sprinklers come on. I close my eyes and let the rain of water wash the sweat and soil from my skin. I open my mouth and let it wet my tongue, begin to quench my thirst.

#

At dinner with Rio, we eat and laugh and talk about nothing, a luxury. When we're done, we kiss goodnight.

Soon I sit in my room with hard copies of the archival documents about Guillermo. I transcribe details from them into a composition I'm writing a half hour at a time before bed, a concise but comprehensive summary of the investigation into his death, written in such a way as to get as much of it as possible onto the network without that old virus deleting it. Even Ramakrishnan's broadcast ended up disappearing briefly from the network because he mentioned Guillermo's real name. Technicians were able to recover most of the rest of the speech, but no matter how hard they work, they can't bring back that one sound byte that pronounces his name.

I've been using a code name which directs the reader to the Archival Office if they want to know who he really was. The code name's descriptor page explains why his real name can't go on the network. It's mostly for historians, educators, people who want to do research, but for everyone else, at least what little of his story is known will be there, even if his name and face can't be. After the crisis, the true repercussions of Midflight won't ever be lost to history, but I find myself driven to ensure this in whatever small way I can.

#

In the morning, the eighth day since my speech, I head toward Pam's lab and pass a modified human in the hallway, green-skinned and wearing tanks of Helena's atmosphere on her back, and a sunlight suit that's likely of her own design, colorful and comfortable-looking. She recognizes me, as most people do now, and smiles. I return the greeting.

I've considered putting all my network profile settings on private, because people from all parts of the ship have started engaging me in conversations both in person and online, and while this is marvelous, it sometime becomes more than I, one person, can respond to It's the opposite of what things must be like for Haruko, whose body is nearly back to normal and who's enjoying a sabbatical from public attention.

But the stories of strangers have been interesting. Most people with a Z chromosome have decided to live, at least for now, with its genes unexpressed, but many want to keep the genes intact in case they should change their minds when we learn more about Helena.

Of those few I've met who choose to continue living with the modifications, all of them do so for different reasons. The Children of Midflight may tell one story, but the current generation refuses to be narrowly defined. Maybe later I'll get in touch with that woman I just saw, and find out what her story is, what kind of person she wants to be.

I walk into Pam's lab, and she grins, those crow's feet spreading.

"I wasn't sure I'd see you again," she says. She stands up from her workstation.

"I wondered myself," I say. I look around at the equipment, the simulator. "I missed this. How long have you been back in the lab?"

"A couple days. But there are data aplenty. Feel like some reading?"

"I'd love it. Anything but another video about the crisis."

"Even you got sick of that, I see."

I sit at a workstation and open up lab reports and spreadsheets of raw data. "I'll watch more of them at some point. I care what people have to say. But three, four hundred messages later, my mind is fried."

"I saw your mother on the network yesterday. Said she was trying to view every one."

"And that's why I'm here and not a career lawmaker," I say. "I can speak my mind when necessary, but focus on finding out new things."

"It's nice, isn't it?" She chuckles. For the rest of the day, we turn our attention to learning.

#

In my dreams I feel the *Euclid* turn. She adjusts her orbit, angling upward from the planet so as not to lose altitude. A burst of speed to prevent orbital decay, maybe seen below by some miniscule fishlike vertebrate as it leaps from the ocean, a quick flash in the sky indistinguishable from a falling star. But orbit, if truly stable, goes on forever. This shooting star, for better or worse, mother to her inhabitants or child, here to observe or to colonize, light years from her source and perhaps millennia from her destination, this star never stops falling.

About the Author

James Dunham's stories have appeared in *The Southeast Review, Crab Fat Magazine, Philadelphia Stories*, and other publications. This is his first published novel. He earned his MFA in fiction from Bowling Green State University and is a graduate of the Writers Institute at Susquehanna University. He is also the editor of the online literary magazine *The Quiet Circle*. He lives in New Jersey with his wife.

Other Books from Lillicat Publishers

Visions VI
GALAXIES

VISIONS V
MILKY WAY

VISIONS V

MILKY WAY

EDITED BY CARROL FIX

VISIONS IV
SPACE BETWEEN STARS

VISIONS III
INSIDE THE KUIPER BELT

VISIONS III

INSIDE THE KUIPER BELT

EDITED BY CARROL FIX

VISIONS II
MOONS OF SATURN

VISIONS

LEAVING EARTH

. . . and coming soon!

Visions VII: Universe